THIEF

Aaron Grunn

Also By Aaron Grunn

Soldiers Die

High School Freak

Alaskan Rivers of Blood

Alternative Book Press
2 Timber Lane
Suite 301
Marlboro, NJ 07746
www.alternativebookpress.com

2014 Paperback Edition

Originally published in electronic form in the United States by Eiso Publishing
Library of Congress Cataloging-in-Publication Data

Aaron, Grunn, [date]
Thief/ by Aaron, Grunn.—1st ed.
p. cm.
1. Thrillers (Fiction). I Title.
PN3311-3503.G786T45   2013
813'.6—dc23
2014933618

ISBN 978-1-940122-09-0
Printed in the United States of America
10 9 8 7 6 5 4 3 2 1

Dedicated to all the sticky fingers out there

The woman stepped out of the taxi, sidestepping the garbage bags on the sidewalk. As she turned the corner, she kicked off her high heels. The sight of the house made her insides twitch. Her backpack dug into her shoulders. She pulled out her cellphone. Outside the house a head inside a car move with crisp movements that spoke of military training. Her heart stopped, and she slowed down. A guard? She'd staked out the house for the past week and hadn't seen any outside guards.

She walked by a brownstone with some well dressed twenty-somethings lounging outside. Next she passed a new silver-colored apartment building. She didn't care for New York's architecture. She very much preferred Barcelona. But she didn't get to choose. Not in her line of work.

Five seconds later, she saw the headlights on the car turn on. Someone exited the building, entered the car, and drove off.

Who was that? The building was supposed to be empty starting half an hour ago, and ending in an hour. If her intel was wrong, should she carry on? She climbed up the house's stairs set on a brownstone facade.

She looked up and down the street once more and clenched her jaw. She signed the cross on her chest and pressed a button on her cell phone. The explosives were silent. She thought she heard a slight thump, but it was nothing that an untrained civilian would notice. The lights went out and a chorus of dismay arose from the twenty-somethings.

She took a deep breath, and her thoughts grew calm while her heart raced. She put on her night-vision contacts. They were uncomfortable, but after a few blinks, she could see. Slipping on her mask, she stepped up to the front door. She had ten minutes. Ten minutes before someone responded to the alarms in the house. At the front door she jammed her vibrating key into the keyhole. After a few seconds the tumblers aligned and the door opened. The second door was electronic. She stuffed a fitting card into the slot. The card was tied to her phone, which in turn was hooked up by server to a hacking algorithm in another country.

A green light lit, and she went through that door. Inside, the house was baroque with all that she hated with such styles. Cameras stared at her, but through some security flaw, they weren't backed with batteries. She ran up a flight of stairs and down a hallway. At the end was another electronically locked door. She stuck in the card and waited as the algorithm did its magic.

This door took longer, and she could feel her hand sweating as the minute mark passed.

That's when she saw the flashlight on the first floor.

"Hello? Is someone here?" an old voice asked.

Damn, she was *certain* the house should've been empty. She could hear the old man trying light switches. Her throat tightened. If he was here that meant a guard was here too. She tried to see if any of the doors were open on the second floor, but they all seemed closed.

"Jim? You there?" the old man said. The light was shining on the stairs now.

The woman glanced at the card. It was still working. She knew that there were eighteen steps to the second floor. Once he was in the hallway there would be no place to hide. And she didn't like dealing with people face-to-face.

"Hello?"

And she saw the card-light turn green. There were only

two more steps. She opened the door and slid in. She reminded herself that next time she needed to bring something to help neutralize such situations. In the end, it was her skin that mattered.

Placing her ear to the door, she held her breath and listened. The old man was opening doors up and down the hallway. Had he heard her? She turned to survey the room. It was filled with rectangular stands topped with vases and sculptures.

There was an ivory comb, its handle an amazing scene from the Resurrection from 13th century France. And there was a piece of vase from the Byzantine Empire. But she stopped when she saw what she wanted. There in front of her was the vase she'd heard about in stories. It was a sculpture from Babylon. Stolen from the Museum of Baghdad less than a decade ago and considered destroyed. Her heart stopped. This was it. She knew it. Priceless. And the price that less couth people would put on it would be insanely high. A few million at least. Of course she wasn't concerned with price.

She heard a door nearby open and shut. Then the handle on the door to her room started to move. She froze. Where was she going to hide? None of the stands were big enough to hide behind. Sweat trickled from in her armpits.

The click of the electronic bolt unlocking pushed her into action. She couldn't risk a confrontation. The ceiling of the room was pre-war height. In the corner beside the door she wedged herself up, trying not to slip or make a noise. She could feel her heart beat against her ribs and push blood past her ears. She took a deep breath. The light from the flashlight highlighted the Babylonian vase as she edged up. Now her back was against the ceiling, and she tried to hold her position. The tendons in her feet, each on one wall, strained. She wasn't certain how long she was going to be able to stay up here.

The flashlight scanned the room.

The old man shuffled into view. He had a hunched back and a cane. She could see the hairs on the back of his neck, and that his skin was black. There was an earpiece in the left ear. So he had comms with someone. This wasn't good.

The old man's head swiveled as he took in the room.

She held her breath. And she could hear the man's slow and labored breathing. Her own heart slowed down. She willed it to stop. But it kept pounding against her ribcage. Kept trying to get out.

The man backed out of the room. The door shut. She counted a few seconds. Just in case he returned.

But she didn't have more time. She lowered herself back down and walked back to the vase. It was encased by a glass cube with a security system embedded. Fine wires ran across the glass in a web. One attempt to move it and an alarm would go off. The room would seal itself and whoever tried to steal it would be trapped.

She pulled out her cutting tool. Underneath the edge of the glass, where it was attached to the stand it stood upon, was a plastic casing. She sliced that and exposed two wires. She cut them ever so slightly, making sure only to cut the rubber encasing and not the conduit inside. These wires were attached to, underneath the case, an ultra sensitive computer which checked to see if anything was being tampered with.

Out of her pocket, she pulled a small circuit board with two wires and a LCD display. She turned it on and attached the two wires to the ones on the case. With her other hand she pulled out a pen. She twisted it ever so slightly and pressed a button, and welded the LCD's wires to the glass cases'.

The LCD display had a readout of volts. She pressed a few buttons and it flashed red. The circuit board was programmed to keep the electrons in the system at a certain level. It would replace whatever was being run through the glass case wires.

The front door slammed. She heard a handful of

masculine voices speak in gruff tones. She heard the old man speak. Did he give them the all clear? Surely they'd want to know what was wrong with the lights. She heard more talking, like terse orders. This wasn't good. She needed to hurry.

The circuit board flashed green. She pulled out some double-sided tape and stuck some to the wires and the rest on the side of the stand. Her hands freed, she took the welding pen and twisted it again. She pressed a button and on the top corner, started to cut the top face of the glass.

She wanted to get out as soon as possible. She could still hear footsteps downstairs. A few doors opened and closed. Sweat dripped down her forehead; she dabbed it with her forearm.

With one side left to cut, she pulled out a suction handle and placed it on the top of the case. Then she cut the remaining side. Pulling off the cut glass face, she pulled out the vase and from her backpack a case. Carefully, she placed the vase inside and put it in her backpack. The packing material would protect the vase, though not from major trauma, such as a confrontation.

Footsteps thumped downstairs and more doors slammed. Some curt yells jolted her heart into racing again.

She pulled out a small cardboard piece and unfolded it, placing it inside the glass cube case. It was a replica of the real vase. Nothing that could pass a discerning eye, but something that might buy her a little extra time. She placed the glass back and pulled off the LCD circuit board.

Footsteps started to run up the stairs. The shouts were louder now. She walked to the window. It too was electronically wired to trip when opened. She scanned the room one more time. There was a shout just outside the door. She froze.

That was stupid, why did she freeze? She pinched herself and placed two wires, using the welding pen to fuse them to the metal trigger halfway up the window.

This was a simpler security system to defeat. She could taste her heart now and her skin glowed with heat. Making certain the wires were fused and nothing could trip the circuit off, she opened the window.

A shout right outside the door flinched her hand. She opened the window another inch and slid out.

Outside, a cool breeze hit her skin and she felt calm. She slid the window back down, knowing that the wires would be found, but only if someone cared to look.

She looked down. Below was a small alley. And across was a brick wall only a few meters from her. She looked back at the room and saw the door cracking open. No time. She grabbed the ledge she was perched on and let herself down. She made sure her legs were at an angle because there was another window directly below. And with a swing she jumped to the ground.

She landed crouched, the pain in her knees traveled up to her femur and ribcage. She bit her tongue and looked up. There was no movement from the window she'd just leapt from. Here in this alley, she could smell urine and garbage. She found a hole in the fence and crawled out to a side road and, removing her mask, she walked in a brisk but unhurried pace.

She didn't hear any alarms and by the time she hailed a taxi it'd been a minute since she jumped. Her heart was calm, though she was giddy with endorphins. It took a lot of energy to stay alert and keep an eye out for any following cars. Exfil was always the hardest part of any mission.

She switched two more taxis before she walked through the park and made it to her safe house. When she was inside, she made sure that the door was locked before she pulled out and examined the vase. She placed it in a crate, a more assured way to protect it.

With a 9mm pistol she lay in her sleeping bag. In the morning the courier would pick up the case and take it to a boat on the Hudson. From there it would be smuggled out of the country. Until then...

The warmth of her sleeping bag and the drained adrenaline pushed her to sleep before she could switch off her light.

"Jimmy, do you have the file?" the man, bespoke suited, and wingtip shoes shining on his table, yelled into his speakerphone.

"Coming right away sir," said a thin voice on the other side.

The man leaned back on his chair and swiveled to look out at the brick and concrete cliffs outside his window. He was tired, but there something else that had to be done, and soon.

"Here," said a young man in a suit that seemed to stretch to fit him. He was sweating, and he kept his eyes trained down as he placed the manila folder on the desk.

"Christ Jimmy, how many times did I ask for this?"

"I was… Sorry sir."

The man wanted to lash out at someone, and Jimmy, his assistant, was usually a perfect target, but he'd been working long hours lately. And the man knew about stretching people too far. Especially if they were good people, like Jimmy.

"Don't worry Jimmy. You almost done with the Reecher files?"

"Yes sir, one more hour and it should be finished."

The man held up a hand. It was a wretched looking hand with two fingers lost in battles he couldn't even remember anymore.

"Take it easy, all right? Head home, get some rest. Tomorrow might be worse," the man said.

"Yes sir," said Jimmy. And he turned and left.

The man grinned as his assistant made for the elevator without looking back once. He too had been in Jimmy's shoes before.

When Jimmy left, and all that remained was the echo of an elevator-ding, the man got up and looked at the city as the sun dropped low and the shadows covered the asphalt rivers below.

The man let out some air and picked up his phone. He

had to get the ball rolling on the problem in the manila folder right away, but deep down inside something in him was kicking back.

"Matt?" a voice on the other side of the line said.

"What?" the man, Matt, said as he stroked the stubs where his fingers should have been.

"You got it started?"

"I'm getting there. You know we're severely understaffed. And we can't keep working like this. I need more money for the payroll," Matt said.

"We don't have time for this. The video conference call with the board will be in ten minutes. Will you be able to brief them?"

Matt looked down and watched as a man hailed a taxi. He was bundled up. Just the thought of the cold sent a dull pain through Matt's hand. He looked at the three fingers on his hand. When he looked away he could always feel five. And the pain of five. And the pain of his missing joints. What had those battles been for? He couldn't remember. Only that he'd survived. He wondered what his enemies thought of the reasons behind the battles. Perhaps one day he would ask.

"I will," Matt said, when the static on the line seemed to sound impatient.

"I hope so. They want top priority on this."

"Of course," Matt said. He was still thinking about his fingers. Reasons for losing them. They had been top priority too. Now he was thinking about how the reasons didn't matter, but the men who sent him there were more or less the same men on the board of his company.

"You all right Matt?"

"I'm fine," Matt said. He was losing his focus, and in his line of work that was foolish. There'd be time to contemplate when he retired.

"I know the hours have been rough. But the board wanted me to tell you that they're 100% behind you. They love everything about you, and what you've done. Hell, they'd better. You've been bringing in the big bucks. Higher profit margins than ever. They'll never forget that. But you need to get this problem finished. And now."

"Got it," Matt said. He hung up before the man could annoy him anymore.

He looked at the file. Its contents were meager. He had been briefed on it a few hours ago and thought nothing of it. But now that he looked at a grainy photograph of a woman, half her face blocked by a door, the other half showing a bright and beautiful set of eyes, curly black hair, and a smile that reminded him of a woman he once had, he felt a sharp pain in his chest.

There was another photo of an older man. Ex-Special Forces, and ex-intelligence agent—a lot like Matt, in fact. The older man worked with the woman, though the extent of their relationship was not known. They'd only found out about him when they'd traced a call the woman had made. His voice showed up on the database. Information from friends at the NSA who were hooked into every call in the world. For the right price anyone could send an algorithm over to look through their database.

Matt stared at the photo. His stomach rumbled, and his phantom fingers let out a shriek of pain. He recognized the older man, though he couldn't place where.

"Where do I know you from, old friend?" Matt said as he massaged his three fingered hand. "And why did you choose this life? Why piss off the most powerful men in the world?"

And that was the reason the board wanted this man and this woman dead. They'd stolen from some very rich people, and they were going to pay. Matt didn't care for his rich paymaster—beyond the check they provided—but he knew better than to cross them. He picked up a phone.

"Get me operations," Matt said.

"Yessir," said a woman on the line.

16

"Hello?" asked a gruff voice.

"Hey Tim, it's Matt."

"Oh, hi there," the voice said in a softer tone. "What's up? They still got you working?"

"Yep. V-con in a few minutes."

"Damn. New file?"

"Yeah. Woman and old man. XDRUT34827090809FGH. You have it?"

"Yup, just came over. I guess it gets priority," said Tim. "Why the hell is that?"

"They've pissed off some major players, Tim."

Tim clucked. "Money over lives I suppose."

Matt puffed out some air to sound as noncommittal as possible. All lines were being listened to. And even though Matt liked Tim, he wasn't going to berate the board's reasons for doing things.

Tim seemed edgy after the pause. "But I'd choose that too."

"Of course," Matt said. "I need you to start triangulating their position. The man and woman. And how many agents can you get on standby?"

"Will do. About five."

"Good. Start searching the man's history. We need to figure out something in his past that we can use. He was with us."

"Will do," Tim said.

"And don't strike until I give the word," Matt said. "Just locate for now."

"All right," Tim said.

"Also, get legal in on this. In case we can put them away. Interpol should be able to help."

"They should," Tim said, though he sounded incredulous.

"Call me whenever you get information," Matt said.

"Anything else?"

"I'll send a message if there is," Matt said.

He hung up and massaged his hands, thinking about the heist the woman pulled off, allegedly, a few days ago. It'd been at the mansion house of an Texan oil magnate. His house was in the Village of Manhattan, and known to be a veritable fortress. But this woman had pierced his armor like it was nothing. The piece stolen was an old vase from Babylon. Not many people even knew it existed. It'd gone lost from Baghdad after the American invasion.

Matt rubbed his phantom fingers again. In the back of his mind, he knew that the artifact in question had been stolen, and essentially the oil-magnate had bought stolen goods, if he hadn't had it stolen himself. But that wasn't a variable he was allowed to add to the equation. One can't have poor people stealing, can they?

His computer started to ring. Matt answered it.

His screen popped up with ten different faces, all at different stages of decay, but all with piercing eyes.

"Hello gentlemen and women," Matt said awkwardly. "I hope everything has been treating you well."

"The hell it has. You get the bitch and her daddy yet?" the oil magnate, with his Texan-drawl said. "She almost killed one of my most loyal workers. Poor old chap almost had a heart attack,"

"Not yet sir," Matt said. He'd learned to bite his tongue decades ago.

"You started on the case, I hope."

"Yessir," Matt said. "We've started the search. There's not much on the woman, but we'll try to get the old man working with her."

"What sort of time do you think you'll need?" asked a woman. She was a former Russian oligarch's wife. She divorced, got the money, then used it to start an empire of her own. "Can't have these people causing havoc."

No, thought Matt, especially not when it's to your purse. "We'll need a few days to even have an idea about that," said

Matt. "The man worked for us, so we'll be able to find more."

"Make sure you get it done," the oil magnate said. "I want her hung."

Matt chewed his tongue hard enough to release a sweet saliva. "Yessir."

And like that the call was over. Matt made sure his computer was off. He stared at the photo of the woman. He'd have liked to learn more about her and the old man's reasons. But he also knew that the more he knew the more likely it was that they'd catch her.

"Whoever you are, I hope you're smarter than us. I really do," Matt said. He switched off the lights and walked down to the elevator. Tomorrow was going to be a busy day. By then their intel apparatus would be gathering important piece of information, and as the board became clearer, Matt would be forced to move his chess pieces. And it was never fair. The woman and old man's resources couldn't compare to the resources that Matt had.

Passing several guards with desultory nods, Matt walked out of the building into midtown Manhattan. In his head he referred to his building as the Death Star. It wasn't far from the truth.

He considered hailing a taxi and heading back home. But melancholy struck him and he knew he didn't want to be alone. He headed to the nearest subway instead, and took a train to his favorite cafe. They'd be playing go tonight. He'd be able to lose himself in a game that didn't matter, and that would mean the world to him.

She stared at the policeman at the Picadilly station for a few seconds. The policeman spoke into his radio and kept his eye on her. There was something in his look that seemed off. She was used to men staring at her, but those looks usually had a hunger, a level of animal instinct that she either recoiled from, or loved. It all depended on the man. And when they stop looking you'll wish for it again. She remembered that from an old woman during her childhood. Who warned her, as she entered her teenage years, that everything between her and her male friends would be different. The old woman had been right.

She adjusted her suit and walked by the policeman. He smiled at her. She smiled back. The animal in his eyes returned, and she felt more comfortable. Outside, the sky was low, gray, and spat out a mist that threatened to wet her hair. She hailed a cab and gave them the address. It was somewhere in Soho.

The flat was on the second floor of a series of mid-rise buildings. She walked in and dropped her bag. It was empty except for the camping equipment she left many years ago. How different she was then. How she appreciated the softer things in life these days. She stretched for a few minutes before she remembered that the British Museum closed in a few hours. Grabbing her jacket, she made sure that the button camera was in place, as was the button in her pocket. She tested it a few times.

Outside she bought some snacks from a corner store, and hailed another taxi.

It took a few minutes before she absorbed where she was at. How many cities had it been in the past month? Twenty? All of them looked the same. Sure, there were minor idiosyncrasies: the languages on the signs were different, here there were double decker buses, the taxis looked quaint, and the skin color of the inhabitants shaded differently. But in the end they looked the same. Skin color didn't change the fact that everyone dressed the same, acted the same, went to the same kind of cafes. She sighed and pulled out a cigarette.

"No smoking ma'am," the driver said.

Well that was one thing different, though she was sure that all the cities would catch up to the Anglo-Saxon obsession with no smoking.

The sky seemed to drop further. Oh yes, and the weather was different as well. She thought back on her time in New York. Her heart rate increased. That had been an exciting moment.

After the taxi wrestled with the traffic, she found herself standing in front of the Roman columns, spread as far as she could see to either side. She walked into the main entrance, passed the apathetic security guards and walked into the grand, centralized, hall. People from all over the world were huddled or craning their necks.

She lingered for a moment, that prickly feeling returning to her extremities. It was subdued compared to the first time she first did this. But it was still there. Perhaps it was the anticipation. Her mind loved the endorphin flow after a properly pulled job. She stared at the ceiling, noting where the cameras were. They wouldn't notice her, but just incase she had a few fake moles, brown colored contacts. And she made sure to stare everyone in the eye.

After a few moments, she made her way to the Egyptian section. Noting the statues from thousands of years ago. Artisans reaching across a cultural and time divide and speaking to the need to create. She sighed. She'd rather have been an artist. But some people didn't have the choice.

She moved on the Middle East section. She paused at the plates with Arabic scripture. Written language. How prevalent it was now, and yet how no one truly knew its origins. How that first man decided that words in the air just simply weren't enough. And he made the first mark. The art, then the words, then... Well that was it, wasn't it? She pursed her lips and made note of the security guards. They wore blue uniforms with minimal insignia, outside of the museum crest. She wondered what sort of training they had. They were all probably underpaid and given no more training than how to use a radio, tell people not to use their cameras, and to step back.

She smiled at one security guard: an older white man with hair growing fiercely out of his ears. He seemed rather nice. Even reminded her of a man she knew as a child. She wondered what this man did in his hours after work. A few tourists, armed with SLR cameras raised them to take photos and were cut down by several security guards' words of reprimand, cooed through smiles.

Everything was as it normally was, she told herself as she inhaled deeply. She noted the cameras on the ceilings and kept away from them. The cameras were what mattered. Somewhere in the security hierarchy, there were people who knew what they were doing. They were most likely on the other end of the radios or cameras, or both. And those were the ones she needed to be wary of.

As she loitered, a man, with chiseled jaw, tanned skin, and sparkling eyes smiled at her. She stopped. Something about him seemed familiar. She looked again until she was certain he was no one she knew. When he caught her looking, he smiled. She knew better than to reciprocate. She was here to work. And yet something about him was giving her a case of deja vu. She shook herself, and reminded herself about the job.

She walked on to the classical Greek section. This was it. And she could feel the change in the air around her as she stepped inside. Alert, she moved her hand into her pocket and made sure to glance down only one more time to make sure that the button camera was pointing in the right direction.

And she walked around taking photos of the entrance to the room. The statues around it. She made notes on the ceilings. She wouldn't get blueprints of the place until tomorrow. Two security guards and two cameras. Slowly, she made her way to the statue. She made certain to spend as much time with the other pieces as with the one she cared about. And she took photos. Noted the glass encasing. Saw the small cut in the felt bottom. A weight sensitive alarm. This wasn't going to be easy.

A rush of the memory of Oslo hit her. It was an easy target, and the security there was laughable compared to here. Though she loved the Scandinavians and their relaxed attitude.

The statue itself wasn't whole: it was a piece of a greater piece that had been blown off the Parthenon several centuries ago. The crumbled white rock, with hints of anthro-smoothness, was beautiful in its own way. It was the torso of a woman. The picture next to the statue showed what the whole woman would look like. Its beauty hit her; her throat contracted.

A few more photos and she walked on to the next statue. She made sure to stay a few minutes longer before she made her way to another room. By this time the sweat in her armpits was dripping down her sides. A few deep breaths, and she left.

"Excuse me?"

She was at the exit and two security guards were staring right at her. Surely they didn't see her taking the photos? Her neck throbbed. If they searched her properly, she'd be found out. She may get away, but the job would be over.

"Yes?" she said, as nicely as she could. The two security guards pointed behind her. She turned, balling her hands into fists.

A security guard, out of breath came up to her. "You dropped this." It was the old man with white wiry hair. He was holding out a piece of paper.

She didn't recognize it. "I don't believe that's mine," she said.

"It's yours," the guard said and smiled. His teeth were perfectly in line.

She grabbed the piece of paper, and she noted the name on his tag: "Andy". "Thank you."

She found an Indian place along the corner of a main thoroughfare. The clouds had burst into a steady drizzle and nighttime had fallen. She sat in a corner with a plate of spicy lentils and lamb. The smell of curry drowned out everything else.

This hit wasn't going to be easy. She sighed and stared out to the red lights driving by, smeared by the rain on the window. The kicked drone of water spray off the road filled her with a loneliness she wasn't expecting.

She walked out of the restaurant and a homeless man hobbled up to her.

"Spare some change. Something to eat?"

"Of course," she said and fished through her pockets. She pulled out a 20 pound note. "Here."

"Thank you," the man said, his eyes opening wide. "I'm a veteran, look." He fished out a certificate wrapped in plastic. "See?"

She nodded. "I'm sorry. It's the way of the world, isn't it?"

"I should've chased the wind," the man said, shaking his head and stuffing away his certificate.

She smiled at him. He seemed exceptionally contemplative. "I know. It's something no one tells you when you're young."

"Is that what you do, miss?" He seemed worried.

"I don't know what I do. Just digging my grave, I suppose."

"Aren't we all," he said. "God bless." He hobbled away fast, as if he were worried she'd change her mind.

"All he's going to do is spend the money on drugs, you know that, right?"

She turned to see an old woman, in a fur coat staring at

her with pursed lips, her finger pointing at her.

"Excuse me?" Coral asked, a little perturbed.

"You're helping bad habits."

"You know him?"

"No, but that's what they do."

"So you want to ruin his life, but I'm sure you won't get him a meal, will you?" The anger boiling her blood surprised her.

"He made his bed, let him sleep in it."

Coral took a deep breath. She didn't want to get into an argument, neither did she want to let this woman think that she was right. "You know nothing of this life," she said and walked away before there was a reply.

The memory of the handsome man she saw in the museum dripped through her veins and made her shiver. He had a scar on his face. One that seemed out of place for such a well-kept man. Was that why he seemed to have a gravitas about him? She felt further jolted when she remembered that he had been looking at her like he knew her, and that he knew what she was doing.

Once inside her flat, she wedged a chair against the door and checked all the windows. It was the result of that man. Past days, before she started on this life, it'd have flushed her skin, maybe had her hoping for love. Now there was none of that, only the assumption that something was amiss. The empty fridge reminded her that she'd have to buy groceries. She left the light on in the kitchen. On the sleeping bag, finding the floor cold and hard, she closed her eyes. The dark blue of the inside of her eyelids grew spots. She felt queasy and opened them back up.

What was wrong? She tried to think about the possible reasons. In this job, though it was never bad to err on the paranoid side, she'd learned to judge her body, the things it wanted. She'd also learned the art of meditation. A year in

India and Tibet. Tapped her subconscious enough that she knew how it spoke. And it was telling her something. What, though? She remembered her instructor telling her that inside everyone's head was the path to the real person. Most people spend a lifetime never accessing this.

She came close. How much did that help her?

She decided to call her father.

"Hello?" a thick unplaceable accent answered the phone. She was calling from a new phone. He wouldn't know who she was.

"Father?" she asked, though she knew very well who it was.

"Coral? Shouldn't you be sleeping? You have a long few days ahead of you."

"I couldn't sleep."

A pause. The cackle of static. She knew it was just 1s and 0s, distorted over hundreds of miles, but she could sense its tension.

"What's wrong?" Father was one who could weigh a great many things with the lucidity of an alien. But when it came to her...

"Well... Not anything really, just that..." She wondered what to say.

"Have you been found out?"

"No, nothing like that. I just have an odd feeling bubbling up... It's probably nothing. I just wanted to talk."

"You sure? If there's too much heat don't be afraid of walking away. We can figure out another way."

"I thought they wanted it at week's end?"

"We can negotiate. Your safety is the most important thing."

She liked it when he talked like that. When the businessman in him melted off and revealed the father in him.

"I'll make the call tomorrow," she said. She sensed the slightest disappointment in his voice; she would never want to let him down.

"I think you need the break."

She took that as a slight. "No, I'll be fine. Just wanted to talk," she lied, hoping that he wouldn't tell.

His paused for a little too long.

"We might not get this chance again," she said.

"Don't worry about that."

It was funny how, even though she was an adult and regularly did jobs on her own, she had that feeling that father was someone who looked over her, drew fear from her lungs and blew bravado back in. She still wanted to press into his chest. She fought that urge, scolding herself for being weak.

"All right," she said, his words easing her tension some. She wished him good bye and went to sleep. She only woke up twice at night. Each time she held her breath, trying to listen for an intruder.

In the morning, she walked to the corner store and bought some groceries.

Back in the flat she pulled out her laptop then maps from her suitcase. She placed them on the floor, using her makeup and shoes to keep the corners down. Made a note of where the sculpture was. The flat had a fireplace, which meant she could mark the map as she saw fit. Push came to shove she'd burn everything. She circled it.

She examined the blueprints of the museum. The vents were forty feet above and they'd recently added an alarm system to all the locked vent openings. If only she had someone who worked inside. The recent robberies in Paris had caused the entire continent to tighten their security. And the Brits, or at least the curators of their museums, were notoriously on edge.

Probably because half their items were stolen at the height of their Empire, she thought. It was the only reason she took these jobs.

She pulled out a blank piece of paper and started to write

out what she was going to need for extra information before she started to plan in earnest:

What kind of alarms.

How many after hour security guards.

Closest police force. Sewer system underneath.

Nearest Underground tunnels.

How busy were the surrounding streets at night.

She tapped the pen against the floor. She couldn't think straight. Her body was still crawling with doubt, or something else. She walked outside. It wasn't raining, but the clouds hung low. There was the smell of raindrops, and the beads of water on parked cars told her she just missed the rain. She shook her head. She bought coffee at a small Turkish store and headed back.

If she couldn't think of any more questions to be asked, she'd have to call this. If her mind was freezing up now, there was no way she could pull this off. She wondered how it would be to work with someone else.

"Hi there beautiful."

She snapped her head and stared at the homeless man. He was hunched over with a wet shawl draped on, but he was well spoken. He'd dark gypsy skin, but blue eyes. For some reason he reminded her of the homeless man from the previous night. But she couldn't remember what he looked like. And the paranoia inside her lit up. If it *was* the homeless man from before that'd be too much of a coincidence.

"Have I seen you before?" she asked.

"Are you kidding me, sweetheart? I'd remember *you* if I'd even seen you from a mile away," he said with a grin. His teeth were surprisingly white.

The word sweetheart usually bothered her. She couldn't help but smile back. "Thank you."

"No, thank you," he said.

"You want some money?" she asked.

He shook his head. "Let me just look and enjoy."

She beamed. His mannerisms spoke of a time when he could have his way with any woman.

"And do you have a boyfriend?" he asked.

"No."

"Husband," he said with a raised finger.

"No."

"Oh? You like the women more?"

"No," she said, for some reason flustered.

He stroked his temple. "I don't understand."

"I'm a loner," she said.

"You shouldn't be," he said sadly. "It's a waste."

He must have seen a look on her face because he raised his hands. "I'm sorry. Not my business. As long as you're happy. I'd hate to think of a beautiful thing like you suffering from loneliness."

"I'm fine, thank you though," she said more curtly than intended.

Back in her flat she wondered about what the homeless man had said. She stared at her list. She'd little more information to ask for. Perhaps this would be good. She pulled up her encrypted email and sent off the request. A few seconds later she got a reply: *Will get on it. Is that it?*

That's it.

And she felt a pang in her heart, but she didn't know what it was. She took a nap, hoping that this odd lack of energy was jet lag and nothing more.

She woke up, realizing it was dark, and that she'd a new email. She shook her head and drank her cold coffee. The email said that she would've no help from inside of the museum. Information on the security system would be available in a day. She groaned and walked outside. It was foggy, visibility no more than fifty feet. After a while, spooked by haunting steps that seemed to follow her wherever she went, she hailed a taxi. The driver, with a white turban wrapped around his head stared at her. One of his eyes was white, never moving. The other was gray, the pupil appeared crack, but she wasn't certain if that was possible. His long crooked nose seemed to match the notched scars on his face.

"The museum," she said and waited for him to turn away. She was usually drawn to odd characters. This time, however, she squirmed to break the spell he seemed to have cast on her. Taking in long slow breaths she watched the sleeping city pass by.

She glanced up to realize that the taxi driver was staring at her through the rear view mirror. She wanted to tell him to keep an eye on the road. But when he negotiated a right turn without looking, she kept quiet. "Where are you from?" she asked.

"Punjab." He blinked for the first time.

"Your scars—"

"Indian Army. War."

She paused. "Kashmir?"

"Everywhere."

She knew about India's many insurgencies. "What brings you here?"

"I work here in the summers. Much cooler."

"You still in the army?"

"No."

She felt foolish for trying to pry and she returned to staring at the dark alleys and traffic lights zooming by.

"And you, what do you do?" he asked pointing at the rear view mirror, his cracked gray eye almost quivering.

"Why are you staring at me?" she asked. She was used to men giving her looks, but she felt like he was studying her, like he already knew her. Or perhaps her paranoia was getting out of hand.

"No reason," he said and blinked before returning his eyes to the road.

She relaxed.

"I'm sorry," he said after a long silence. "I just think that there's something about your looks..."

She could feel blood warming her cheeks. "Thank you," she said.

He nodded and returned his eyes to the road.

"The museum is closed," he said.

She looked up and saw that she was in front of the museum. It was just then that she realized that she hadn't told him which museum she wanted. And for a city with many museums, it was impossible that he guessed.

"I just wanted to walk around."

"I know a person who works at security. He can help you take a look around," the man said.

"Let's see," she said and stepped out.

He stepped out with her. There was something about the way he sidled up next to her that made her comfortable. When she glanced up, she realized he was observing her. Her heart jumped, and she wondered why she wasn't being more careful. She pursed her lips and glanced back at the lit facade of the museum.

"It's beautiful at night," he said. "I always wondered why these great cities didn't open their museums all night. Think of all the people who would come."

She nodded though it'd make her job much harder. And yet she was still wary about his stare. She was certain that now it wasn't just the hunger of a man who didn't have much.

"Your name?" he asked.

She stared at a column lit up in front of her.

"You know someone inside?" she asked, then felt immediately stupid since "inside" sounded like she was doing a job—or was that just her paranoia?

He grinned. "I do." He held out his hand. "I'm Taj."

"Pleased to meet you Taj." He seemed genuinely nice.

"I'm only staring because you also seem so smart. And..."

"And what?" she asked. An old couple shuffled by them. They were white with dark wrinkles that mapped their faces.

31

The old woman smiled at them both. Coral wanted to tell her that Taj wasn't her man, since the look was one of those approving ones, but she just smiled back. When the old couple shuffled out of earshot she turned to Taj.

"Well," Taj said, shifting his feet. "Who comes to a museum after it's closed?" He glanced at his hands.

"I thought you said it was beautiful?" She still couldn't read his face. He was pretending to be embarrassed by his own question, and yet his mannerisms until now spoke of a man never bashful.

"It is," he said.

Silence enveloped them. In the distance, somewhere in a dark alley she couldn't see, an eruption of laughter cascaded towards them. For as large as a city as it was, London suddenly seemed lonely to her. She stepped closer to Taj. His eyes were soft, and she could see that he was perturbed by her implied accusations.

"Then?" she asked.

"Something about you is unusual."

"Go on," she said and smiled, hoping to blunt the damage if he did turn out to be innocent.

"I'm not sure. Maybe I'm just getting old. You know they did a study and said that old people lose touch with their senses. They forget how to judge people."

"Oh? So your judgment is off?" she asked, and laughed when Taj flashed a grin.

She touched his arm and his torso crumpled a millimeter. She felt better.

"I'm Caroline," she said. No need for real names.

"Pleasure to meet you," Taj said. "Why isn't someone like you not inside a club somewhere. Basking in young men's showering stares and gifts?"

"That's not my cup of tea, Taj. I'm sure your judgment isn't that far gone."

"Ah, you make fun of me," he said. He sounded more

relaxed. "But you enjoy museums more than drinking?

"Of course," she said. She felt him stand too stiff. She wondered how old he was.

"Do you have a family?" she asked.

"Yes," he said.

She expected to hear more, perhaps boast with some photos, but he didn't say anything else. Was he thinking of getting lucky? She took a step away, then decided that perhaps that's what she would use if she'd to get something from him.

A jet flew overhead.

"You want to see my friend?" Taj asked as he picked out his phone and dialed a number. A few mumbles and greetings later: "Let's go."

They walked towards the same entrance she'd gone up earlier. At the entrance a security guard with a hand-held radio in hand walked up to them. "Taj, you all right?"

"I'm doing great," Taj said and the two embraced. The security guard's skin seemed more pruned.

"Andy, this is Caroline."

Coral shook hands with the security guard. She was certain it was the man from before, though he didn't seem to recognize her. "Pleased to meet you."

Andy grinned and elbowed Taj while winking at Coral. "You old dog. I didn't know you were looking for new blood for your dynasty."

Taj looked shocked, his mouth half-open. "No, no. You know me Andy. I would never." He looked at Andy then back at Coral.

Andy shook his head at Taj. He winked at Coral when Taj wasn't looking. "Come on Taj, you mean to tell me nothing's going on between you two? If you want a room in the museum, just ask."

Carol couldn't help but smile. "Taj, is this true?"

Taj turned thoroughly red, almost purple. "It is not," he said, his voice picking up an octave, and a few decibels. "You know I'd never cheat on my wife." His finger rose and headed for Andy's chest.

"All right, all right," Andy said.

Carol could see the corner of the Englishman's lips turned up.

"If you don't want to tell me that's fine," Andy said. "I thought we were friends. And you know I can keep a secret. Lord knows you have plenty of mine." Andy raised his hands chest level, as if to deflect Taj's finger.

"Andy!" Taj said, his voice returning to its previous low, but this time it was very loud. He turned to Coral. "Caroline, tell him you're only my fare."

Coral saw Andy wink at her again. A giddy feeling inside told her to have some fun. She feigned shock. "Is that what you call it? You're telling me this was nothing?"

Taj froze. He didn't know how to take that. "I-I... I never. I have a wife," he said.

"Yes, we know Taj. It's fine to eat out every now and then," said Andy. "And if you are, you might as well do it someplace fine." Another wink.

Taj was now stepping away from the two of them. His finger had come down. "I did not mean anything by coming out here," he said to Coral. "You must—"

Andy started to laugh, his whole body heaving. Coral grinned. Taj stared at them both.

"Both of you are crazy, you know that?" He turned away.

Andy grabbed his arm. "Oh come on. We're only having a bit of fun. You know that."

Taj jerked Andy's grip off. "I never cheated on my wife."

"Easy," Andy said. "We know that. Don't we?"

"We do," Coral said. "I was only joking, Taj."

Taj's eyes darted between them. "This is no joke."

"I'm sorry," Andy said. He flashed another wink. "So you're just his fare?"

Coral smiled. "I was."

Taj mumbled to himself. "Not once. Always stayed true."

"You two been friends long?" Coral asked.

"Yes. We worked together on a joint mission once, ain't that right Taj?" Andy said.

"We did," Taj said, startled. "And I thought you were a comrade in arms, not someone to slander my name."

Taj still seemed out of it, and yet Andy was grinning like he was used to this.

"What sort of mission?" Coral asked.

"Oh, something out in the deserts of some country," Andy said, waving a hand in the air.

And with a startle in her heart, Coral saw in the flash of his eye a hint of the violence these two men must have committed. Now she saw scars on Andy's face, the back of his hands. She saw that he handled his weight very well. She saw that in Taj too. She had seen military men before, and she liked their presence.

"You worked with the Indian Army?" she asked.

"Oh no, we went Foreign Legion... Better money. Fewer questions," Andy said.

She cocked her head and smiled, trying to feign like she didn't know as much as she did. "Oh?"

"That's right. We're a couple of veterans," Andy said puffing out his chest.

Taj smiled. He seemed to have forgotten his friend's slights.

"He's right. After the Indian Army I realized that there wouldn't be any chance at promotion and the family needed more money."

He spoke in a strained voice; perhaps he was lying. As far as she knew, most people who joined the Foreign Legion were criminals. People looking to erase their past.

"Well, I think the world of military men," she said. "But why take *these* jobs afterwards?"

Both men looked down at their feet, shuffling their

weight.

"You know how it is," said Andy. "You charge forth to the breach as a young man. You get lucky—"

"Or maybe unlucky," Taj said, raising his long forefinger again.

"And you live. Then you're too old to charge. And they can't use you. But you get out and the real world can't use you either," Andy said. "So I did what I could. I've a family. I don't see them much, but I like to help them out."

Taj nodded. The light of the museum shifted in his eyes. Were those tears? "Don't see mine. Years of fighting saw to that. But we can at least help them out."

Coral wondered why he was so sensitive about cheating on his wife. She tried to show her saddest face, and she touched each of them on the arm. Inside, she was bubbling with joy. Two disgruntled men who looked like they could use some money. And they weren't quite family men.

Andy led them to the front. Another security guard slept on the desk.

"Leave him be," Andy said. "The hours here are shit, and they don't pay enough."

Coral smiled. "And you're the boss here?"

"On the ground I'm the boss. So basically all calls come through me. If I can't handle it, it goes up to the head honcho."

"Who's that?" she asked, trying to be as nonchalant as possible.

"Oh, some suit," Andy said, again waving his hand.

They walked down the halls. "As you can see, the place is deserted. These days they don't need so many people. All they have are these high class security systems."

"So the security guards can't just walk out with the goods," Coral said, fluttering her eyelashes at Andy.

"Oh, you're dangerous. You're lucky I'm not younger," Andy said and looked at Taj.

Taj shook his head.

"But right you are," Andy said. "They've everything recorded. In the morning the curators're supposed to run through and make sure everything's in place."

Taj craned his neck, enthralled with the museum.

"You've been here before?" Coral asked him.

"No. This is the first time. Usually I just pick him up to go to the pub," Taj said.

Their footsteps echoed down a hallway. The harshness of the marble floors underneath was amplified in the abandoned building. The aroma of polish and canvas enveloped her, and she instinctively hooked her arm into Andy's. Andy didn't miss a stride and placed a hand on her elbow.

"And they probably have someone else looking at these cameras too?" she said.

"No." Andy threw his shoulders back and made a majestic arch with his arm. "They're supposed to have another set of guards looking at them, but they don't anymore. Technically we're not allowed to walk down here."

"Why?"

"No reason. But if we get too close to any of the paintings or sculptures, the motion-sensor is more sensitive at night."

Taj walked up behind them. "Can't believe they think replacing people with robots will work," he said.

"It works sometimes," Coral said, trying to play devil's advocate to better cover her true intentions.

"Right. When the thieves do exactly what the machine wants them to. Anything else, and..." Andy said and made a slashing movement with his hand.

She made sure to stay away from the room she'd observed earlier. Silence reigned for a few minutes so she spoke up: "So do you have photos of your families?"

Taj pulled out his wallet and showed a picture of him, younger, with a young man and old woman.

"Only son?" she asked.

Taj nodded.

"He's handsome," she said.

Taj smiled. "Thank you."

"Takes after his old man."

Taj flinched and Coral wondered if he was sensitive to the commonality of time.

"Here's mine," Andy said.

There was an old picture of a young woman and two girls in their teens.

"They're young," she said.

"I know," Andy said, his face twisting. "The ex won't give me a new photo. It's her way of punishing me."

"Twins?"

"Yep," Andy said.

"In college?" she asked.

"Just finished," he said. "I try to help them out with money. That's all they'll take." He seemed brittle all of a sudden.

"You don't get to see them?" she asked.

"They don't care for me. They'd rather spend time with their step-father. He's more money than me."

Coral felt a lurch in her heart.

"You get to see yours?" Coral asked Taj.

"I do," Taj said. "But all the words she filled him with means he doesn't care to see me much."

"I'm sure they care, sometimes it's hard to get it across," she said.

Taj stared hard at his shoes. He didn't look like he believed her.

"How about you?" Andy asked, stuffing the photos away.

"No family," she said, wondering how much she should tell them.

"None?" Andy said, his forehead breaking out into multiple lines.

"I was adopted," she said. "My real parents I never knew. Don't know much about them even now."

"What do you do?" Taj asked.

Even though she felt a connection with each of them, she could feel paranoia creeping up her brain. Her stomach rumbled. Something was wrong.

"Let's go to a pub," Andy said. Taj nodded in agreement.

His smile was genuine and though she didn't trust him entirely, she didn't want to be alone in her unfurnished safe house.

"Fine," she said. "Don't you have to get back to your shift?"

Andy rolled his eyes. "Don't worry about that."

That seemed odd too, but she ignored the rumblings in her stomach. They got in the taxi, her in the back, and drove off.

"I know just the place near where I live," said Andy.

Coral watched as the city zipped by: taillights and groups of debauchery. In some neighborhoods a hint of cumin and curry stunk up the air.

The pub was a dark hole on the southern edge of the Soho district. It was skinny with room only for a bar and stools. Only a handful of customers surrounded the bar. The three of them nestled on the first three stools.

A bartender, bald head, big belly, and full sleeve tattoos spilling from his sleeveless shirt came up to them. He had a glass eye and a limp.

"Three pints," Andy said.

Taj coughed and looked at Coral.

"Oh, sorry," Andy said. "What will you have?"

"Just a water," she said.

The bartender stared at her. She felt that they'd met somewhere else in life, or perhaps they both saw something of the work each did. She held his stare until he moved off.

"Don't mind him," Taj said. "He looks rough, but he has

a heart of gold."

"I'm sure he does," Coral said, wondering if Taj and Andy were just naive and perhaps that's why they got to this point in life.

"Taj, Andy! How goes it?"

A young man walked in. He shook his umbrella, drops gleamed off the barlight and fell to the floor.

"Raining already?" asked Taj.

"That's right," said the young man.

As he stepped into the soft glow of the bar's light, Coral had to hold her breath. He was tall, with dark hair and olive skin, and his eyes seemed to twinkle when they saw her. He too froze.

The bartender slammed down three pints of beer. "A pint for you Drake?"

"Please," the young man said.

Coral felt thankful for the respite, though she wanted to ask for a water to test the bartender. The young man smiled at her again. She could see a scar on his cheek. His aura was sucking the air out of her lungs. She leaned in to get a better look. Taj and Andy seemed to be statues, and she just barely caught them exchanging a look.

The bartender slammed another beer down. Some froth landed on Coral's cheek. She glanced over.

"Easy with the pints," Taj said. "You're not artillery."

The bartender barked and walked back into the shadows.

"Where are my manners," said Drake. "I'm Drake." He stuck out his hand.

"I'm Caroline," she said, only remembering the fake name she'd used at the last second. "What do you do?"

"I'm a writer. You?"

She forgot what she'd said. "I'm here visiting." She felt the pause of awkwardness. "And what do you write?"

"Thrillers. Well," the man brushed his chin. "That's what pays the bills. My heart's in odd post-modern pieces that shed a little bit of light on our condition."

"Don't start with that talk," Andy said, taking a sip of his pint, then handing out everyone else's drinks. "For a second I thought he had you beat," Andy said and winked at Coral. "Until he started with that uppity nonsense."

"Enough from you," Taj said.

"It's fine," Coral said. She could feel all her unease from earlier evaporate. But she couldn't help staring at Drake.

"Excuse me a moment," she said and headed to the john. It was co-ed, and without a lock. Inside she could hardly breath. The stench of old urine hung on her tongue. She took a deep breath and checked her phone. Nothing. It wasn't normal to have received nothing in reply to her requests.

She sent a few more texts before she walked back out.

Taj and Andy were laughing about something. It seemed to be at Drake's expense. When she sat back on her stool, the three of them fell silent.

"What are you three conspiring about?"

"Nothing," said Taj.

She tried to keep her eyes on him and not flutter over to Drake. His pull was overpowering. It wasn't his handsome looks, but just the way he carried himself.

Taj and Andy went back and forth about the recent spate of stabbings in South London.

"It's those Jamaican chaps," Andy said. "They're always up to no good."

"Anything you say," Taj said. "They're poor, what can you expect? This is Thatcher's legacy. We leave enough people behind and the whole system falls down."

"What do you think?" Coral asked Drake. She knew it would result in him asking her questions that she wouldn't necessarily be able to answer, but she'd to break into his head just a little more.

"Poverty is definitely a powerful motivator in these cases. I'd say gang warfare is just another symptom. It sounds bad, but only because we've had it so good. One need only remember how bad things were in Victorian-era London. Murders like this were commonplace back then."

She liked him, and she tried hard not to smile. "That sounds like a level-headed analysis. You've always been a write?" she asked.

"I've held a few other jobs," he said.

She could feel his eyes dance over her face. But it wasn't lust. It was a very methodical look.

"Well, look at the time," Taj said and kicked Andy.

"What?" Andy said. He seemed to be knocked out of a daze. "What are you talking about? It's hardly late."

Taj leaned past Coral and threw some money down on the bar. "It's time for us to go old friend. Let's exchange numbers, and stay in touch," Taj said to her.

"I'm sure I don't need to be told when my bedtime is," said Andy to himself more than anyone else.

Taj grabbed his elbow. "Let's go, you've had too much." He pulled Andy with him and out the door.

"What the hell is wrong with you, you turban wearin—"

The door slammed shut.

Drake grinned.

Coral had always been one to protect her heart. And she'd been taught to always keep men back. It'd never been hard. Yet now, as she smelled his cologne and clean clothes, she couldn't help dreaming about a future with him.

"What are you writing now?" she asked.

"Trying to finish up a thriller about an MI6 agent working in Syria."

"Do you travel to get close to your subjects?"

"I do," he said. His hand went up to his scar. "This was from a fight outside Damascus."

"You fought?" she asked.

"Got caught in a fight is more like it."

"Never been one for violence," she said.

"Neither have I. Well at least not since my time in the Army."

"British?"

"That's what they said."

She smiled, a warmth growing and spreading in her chest matched the butterflies in her stomach. She sat there, absorbing his presence. And he too stood still. There was nothing awkward about this silence. Her heart raced.

"I'd better be getting back to my place," she said, glancing at her watch.

"Why?"

"I've work to do."

"I thought you were just visiting."

She felt bad for lying to him, but reminded herself that it was needed. "There's always work." Her face grew warm.

He didn't seem to believe her.

"Where are you staying?" he asked.

"North of Paddington."

"That's far."

"Perhaps."

"Better get going then," he said and glanced at the door.

She sensed a teasing in his voice and it annoyed her. They walked outside where it was raining again. It seemed restrictive, this rain, but the smell of a constantly clean city was something she was learning to like.

"Here," he said holding out his umbrella.

"No."

"Take it. I live only a few blocks away," he said.

They stood under the bar's awning staring at each other. Again there was something about him that made such silence perfect.

"I've extra at my place," he said.

She pulled out her phone. "Sorry I've a close friend who hasn't called all day," she said. She knew it sounded off, but she felt as if he wouldn't mind. "My stomach tells me that something is wrong."

"Sorry."

She didn't realize it, but they were walking together. To his place, she assumed.

"I'm rarely scared. But I am now," she said still staring at her phone. They were standing in front of some steps.

"It's all right to be scared. And it's all right to trust your gut instinct."

They walked through the front door and into a hallway that smelled of curry.

"My neighbors," he said wrinkling his nose. "You can stay."

"I just don't want to be alone." She liked that he appeared to be able to read her mind.

"I know the feeling," he said.

"Don't try anything funny." She smirked.

He shook his head as he looked at the ground. They walked into his apartment. A cat greeted them.

"Sofie," he said. "Meet Caroline."

"It's Coral," she said.

He cocked his head.

"Sorry. I suppose I should be honest with you."

He reached down and pet the cat. He showed her his bedroom. "You can sleep here. I'll be on the floor in the living room."

"No. You don't have to do that for me."

"I'm military and I actually prefer the floor. No discussion. You want something to eat?" he said as he walked back to the kitchen area.

"I'm fine."

She didn't realize how tired she was until she woke up from a nightmare in the middle of the night. She tried to call him, but there was no answer.

She realized that the cat was sleeping near her head. She went to the living room.

Drake shuffled on the floor. "What is it? Sofie wake you up?"

"No. I'm certain something happened to my friend."

"Where does he live?"

"Crete."

"That's a long way."

"It is."

"What are you doing here?" he asked.

"I don't know if I can tell you that yet..." she said, garnering no response from his face. She imagined that he was a great poker player. "Were you ever scared in the military?"

"I'd a few moments when I was caught out in Basra, alone and in civvies. An ambush that almost got me. I drove like a madman and got out though... My interpreter was an amazing guy." His voice had dropped a few octaves.

She wondered what unit she was with. "What about gut feelings?"

"Follow them when there's nothing else. But mine tend to be wrong."

"My friend and I work in a very dangerous business," she said, now scared that she was so willing to open up to a stranger and yet feeling so comfortable too. "I think his time, and maybe mine, has run out."

Drake didn't say anything. Sofie jumped between them and meowed. Coral could smell the meat off the cat's breath. Her mind twisted tight. And she knew that she had to leave tonight. Something in the air, in the sound of the cars passing in the wet street, told her that London wasn't safe anymore.

Matt finished his game of go. It was an early loss. He'd fallen back to his old mistakes of holding on to groups of stones that were beyond saving. Then after spending too much effort in one corner, he would turn his attention to another corner and fight with all his tactical might. But soon he would realize that his crafty opponent, a short Korean girl in her teens from Seoul with darting eyes and a scar on her cheek that she always tried to cover with too much makeup, was consolidating the other corners. He was actually fighting himself. He'd try to salvage some territory, but it'd cost more stones that she encircled and gulped up. She smiled at the end, rocking at the edge of her chair. Matt found it hard to be angry.

"Next time I give you five stones," she said, referring to the handicap given to inferior players. She seemed to realize her slight. "Sorry... No."

Matt wasn't sure what she was saying no to, but he knew she must have violated some Korean social more about talking down to elders.

"No," he said. "It's okay. You play very well. I just had a bad day. I'll play you again next week, okay?" He knew that he couldn't make such promises with his time, but he wanted to feel normal, of only for a second.

"Of course," she said. Her eyes, from behind her thick glasses, met his for a second and she smiled, blushed, stared at the board. She was pretty, and if Matt were younger he'd have seized this opportunity. But he decided that he would rather guide her than trick her. He thought again about the woman he was being paid to chase. A glance at his phone told him that nothing had been found out yet.

"Maybe next time you can teach me something," he said.

She smiled. In a minute she'd cleared out the board and was going over the game. That she could recount the exact placement of three hundred stones was nothing short of amazing, and he smiled and watched in awe as she dissected his pathetic game.

"And here you played here. Not good," she said.

He stared. She was right. He was horrible at this game of strategy; chess was much easier. "And how would you have played?" he asked. His mind once again flew to the woman in the file. He'd seen the videos of the oil-magnate's house in Manhattan as she robbed it. The woman was good. Maybe great. The chatter he'd heard about her was that she was too smart to have any outstanding warrants on her. Same with her boss, or father, or what have you.

As the Korean girl pointed out the sane strategy, Matt wondered what could have driven the woman he was chasing into the life she was living.

"Sorry but what was your name?"

"Huh?" Matt asked. His knees felt tight, and as he shook out his legs they made a popping sound that reminded him of his age.

"Your name?" the Korean girl asked.

"Matt, you?"

"Jay."

Matt smiled as he shook her hand. He knew Jay wasn't her name and in fact was the girl's way of saying that her name was too complicated for a round-eye like him to pronounce so she was going to just give him something simple that he could pronounce rather than embarrassing both of them.

"Nice to meet you," she said, smiling. She now held his stare, enough that it stirred his insides.

"What do you do here?" he asked, not sure if he was going to answer the reciprocal question.

"I'm a student. Math department."

"Nice," he said, his head racing for a decent way to cover up his job.

"You?"

"I'm a business man. I work with imports," he said, hoping it would end there.

47

"What kind?" she said, her eyes pierced through him.

"Anything that pays." He hoped she would go back to the go board. He shifted in his seat. He could still feel her eyes on him. Glancing around he took in the handful of other go players hunched over boards sprinkled among the normal coffee drinkers who were chatting and holding cups to their faces.

"Interesting," said Jay. She returned to destroying his go abilities. He chewed the inside of his cheek each time she showed him how horribly he had played.

A few minutes later he excused himself. There'd be many sleepless nights to come. He might as well catch up on sleep while he could.

Back in his apartment on 23rd street, he lowered all his blinds and switched on his bedroom light. He considered having a shower, but collapsed on his bed, thinking about what he was going to do about the woman. He'd never before wanted to let go of a suspect they were chasing. Never. And yet with this woman, with what he knew of her story, he did. It was because she made him feel dirty. With that thought, and a glass of whiskey, he went to sleep.

He awoke at 2 am, his phone ringing, vibrating, tickling his pelvic bone. He dismissed the call and rolled over. The phone started again. He pulled it out and stared at the number. It was the office. Christ, had they already started?

"Hello?" Matt said.

"Matt?"

"Tim? You still up?"

"Yeah. There was a lead... On the old man."

Matt felt his heart tighten. He didn't want to hear this. He'd worked long enough with Tim, his bloodhound, to hear the tone in his voice that indicated a found quarry.

"Nice," Matt forced himself to say. "You have an address?"

"Address, cellphone, the whole lot," said Tim.

"Cell?" Matt asked. He remembered that old man had dropped his cell phone the moment they'd tracked it once before.

"Yeah, a virtual tracker on it. NSA has a new system—"

"They're letting us use it?" Matt asked, almost angry that they would be willing to give a private company that kind of information.

"Yeah, I know a few people," Tim said.

"Of course. So where is the old man? Is he moving?"

"No. He's staying put."

It sounded like Tim was sitting on something.

"Good then, I'll—"

"You're not going to like it, but the oil-magnate fuck called in."

"What?" Matt asked, anger rising inside him. The oil-magnate may have been a co-owner of the company, but there was no way he'd interfere with the inner workings of a mission. "How'd he know?"

"He owns us, remember?" Tim said.

Matt didn't say anything.

"He must have told someone to call him, Matt. It wasn't me. Believe me. I hate talking to that slimey toad."

"I know. It *is* his show... Still. What did he do?"

"He wants. No, he ordered that The Coyote does this job."

The Coyote. There was a name that Matt hoped to never hear again in his lifetime. Not after the time in Sierra Leone. "Why the hell does he want that screw ball?"

"Said he's the only one with the chops for the job."

"What does he know about these jobs?" A small voice in the back of Matt's head reminded him that he was talking to an office phone and the old oil-magnate may very well have tapped these.

"Hey, speaking to the choir bud, but I gotta listen to the

boss."

"Sure. Have you called him in already?"

"Yup," said Tim.

"Where's the suspect located?"

"Greece. Crete. I can send you the information."

"Coyote already there?"

"He's eight hours out."

Matt reached into his pockets and felt a stone from the game of go he'd been playing. He pulled it out and rubbed it over in his palm. Eight hours out. He wasn't certain he wanted to do something about this. His bosses wanted it done this way, so what choice did he have? "Do they have the girl's location yet?"

A long pause and Matt realized that he'd used the word "they" and Tim must have realized the same thing too.

"No. *We* don't. But I'm sure The Coyote will get it off the old man."

"I'm sure he will," Matt said. "Let me know when we go live, all right?"

"Sure thing," Tim said and hung up.

Matt stared at the black go stone. He suddenly didn't want to be alone. He kicked himself, remembering that in this career it was better to have few attachments. He threw the stone across the room. "Well, old man. I hope you haven't been just lucky so far, and you're good enough know when to run." He could feel goose bumps forming.

Matt put on his running gear. It was late, but he needed something to clear his head. Outside, the cold air nipped at his neck and throat. He ran up and down the avenue, drunk onlookers and city construction workers giving him odd looks. He could smell the crisp air sandwiched with dirty water and settling pollution. And still he couldn't help but think about the woman and how he hoped she'd be able to escape the dragnet soon to be thrown over her. On the leg back, he ran as fast as he could. His legs were strong, but his chest almost caved in as he tried to suck in air, pumping his hands and hoping to pass out. His heart felt weak. Long hours at a desk had melted away his athleticism and his sense of immortality.

Back at his building, panting for air, he felt an odd sickness taking over. He walked into his bathroom and turned on the shower.

When he was clean and dry, Matt put on a pair of jeans with a sports jacket and ran out of his apartment building. He made a detour to get some food, but he was back in his office before the sky cracked open into light.

"Tim," Matt said into his phone.

"You back in the office?" Tim said. He sounded distant.

"Where's Coyote?"

"You've got good timing. It's about to go live. I'll send the link."

Matt switched on his computer and typed in his password. In a few seconds the screen flickered to life, and he saw the all-green top down view of a house on the beach. In the corner of the screen was the splash of the sea. And in the house was the thermal image of a man sleeping. Or breathing steadily in his bed. The computer read out indicated an 80% chance that the man was actually asleep.

A car pulled up. A man stepped out, craning his neck to take in his surroundings. He pulled out a silenced handgun. And he walked to the house.

Even with this aerial view from miles in the sky, Matt could tell The Coyote's signature walk. He could see the limp from the shrapnel the operator had received in Iraq. Matt's heart beat faster.

The Coyote walked up to the front door. He checked some bushes. Then he checked the door. Matt could see the man jiggling the door, probably working his magic to get the door to open. Matt hoped that the old man inside would be able to hear it.

But no luck, Coyote was inside. He made his way to the

bedroom. The thermal body kept on sleeping.

Then the old man stirred. The Coyote was standing right in front of the old man now and leaned over him with a needle in his hand. The needle pressed into the old man. The old man jerked forward and leapt out of bed.

The Coyote pointed his gun at the man. It was hard to tell with a thermal view, but chances were that the old man could barely make out the dark figure in front of him. And the serum in the needle was just about to take effect. The old man fell and was soon twitching.

Matt could feel his throat tighten. He didn't want to see this happen, but he knew The Coyote and knew the SOB enjoyed this part the most. A few seconds later the old man was tied, each limb to a bedpost. The Coyote stripped him and turned on the radio. Matt could hear the short breaths of the old man. He could almost smell his fear.

"Name please," said Coyote's stern but thin voice.

The old man was still gathering his wits.

"I said," Coyote said, and leaned over with a knife. "Name!"

The old man let out a cry. Matt could see the thermal spill. Blood. Perhaps there was hope that the old man wouldn't last long.

"Fuck you," said the old man. His voice was gravelly, worn out.

Matt chuckled and sighed: "You've got balls old man. But that was stupid."

"Oh?" Coyote said, raising his knife again.

Matt closed his eyes. He thought about switching off the computer.

"Oh no," Coyote said.

Matt opened his eyes. Coyote was standing over the old man and appeared to be shaking him. Was the old man dead already? Coyote reached into the old man's mouth.

"A damn pill," the Coyote said after a small struggle. "He

had a pill in his mouth." There was only disappointment in his voice.

A few seconds later. "He's dead," said Coyote. That was it. The figure walked around the house throwing in anything that the quants back here would be able to sift through for information—hard drives, phones, papers, pictures—then threw an incendiary grenade as he walked out.

The car drove away. A few seconds later there was a thermal burst inside the house. Soon the pulsating glow had spread over the whole house. The old man's body twitched, but Matt knew it was only the heat. Soon the whole house was a massive glow. The picture cut out.

Matt leaned back in his chair. "Well old man, you managed to escape pain." Matt had to wonder why it was that a thief had a pill in his mouth. That was some level of discipline not known to most thieves. Was it possible this old man was foreign intelligence? He lay down on the floor next to his desk and rested his head on his arm. He'd get some sleep for now, because this mission just became that much more complicated.

He closed his eyes. For some reason a part of his brain didn't want to go to sleep. The motion sensing lights clicked off. Light from outside filtered in from the window. The light indicated the cloudy kind of day he hated. He could smell the dust off the floor. He tried to close his eyes, a reddish-blue color covering his world. And the thermal scene of the old man being murdered appeared. His heart beat faster. He'd seen thousands of such kills. Thermal and otherwise. And still this one affected him the most. The image crawled into his brain, playing over and over.

He rolled to his side. The fetal position now. It was interesting to view his office from the floor. He could see the dirty underside of his desk.

His mind flinched, flashing the thermal shot of the old man. The scream. He smelled something—cologne?—that wasn't his scent. And his eye caught a form in the corner of the underbelly of his desk.

He sat up and shuffled over. His knees and hips were tight from running and popped a few times. Using his phone's light, he checked out the contraption. It was a listening device. Another wire led to the back of his drawer. Batteries. Which meant it was constantly sending signals. He stared at it. His entire phone call had been heard.

He sat back on his chair, his mind tightening as he tried to think of who would do this. The Texan oil-magnate could have. But he didn't see why. He dismissed the thought of another in the company spying on him. No one he knew had the balls to do this. It could have been another private intelligence agency trying to get the jump on them. Or a foreign intelligence agency. His mind flashed to the old man and the pill in his mouth. Did *he* know?

Matt started to do some breathing exercises. He'd to control his thoughts. The normal protocol was to call internal security and have them sweep his office, his apartment for any other bugs. But he didn't want to. He relaxed his head on his desk. It'd been too stressful a day. And all evidence pointed to a more stressful week.

Again, his mind refused to worry about the bug and instead settled on the thermal image of the old man tied to the bed. So many moments like these in his life. But this time he was certain he'd been pushed to the limit. Why? The old man was no saint. Not from the information Matt'd read about him.

Another thought flashed across Matt's mind: perhaps he could quit. He'd enough saved up. No, he reminded himself. His parents in Michigan were both ailing, their Social Security checks were meager replacements for a life of toil, and their 401ks had been raided by their respective companies before they went bankrupt. They needed him for the money. He remembered innocent days in Michigan, cutting school early to go smoke weed in the city park. He missed that. He'd fallen so far since then.

A tremor ran through his muscles. He could feel a sting in his eyes. It was moments like these where he wished he prayed.

He closed his eyes, and this time he fell asleep.

He was on a beach, a figure coming towards him. As the figure came closer, he could see it was a woman. He was certain he could recognize it. An old cut in his heart reopened. The woman walked up to him. He tried to sit up and greet her, but he was too tired. The sun was beating down on him, rays piercing through the palm tree above him and lasing through his skin. Sweat dripped down his forehead. He tried to touch her face, but he'd no energy. She placed her hand on his face. "Go to sleep," she whispered. He felt her shaking his head. He was certain he knew her.

"You asleep?"

Matt lurched up and saw Tim staring at him.

"Crap, what time is it?" Matt said, rubbing a piece of grime out of his eyes. His throat was parched, and he couldn't remember a dream he just had, though he felt like it was still in his DNA, still making him groggy and unwilling to face reality.

"It's ten in the morning. We've been trying to call you all day. They analyzed the information from the old man's house."

Matt's heart dropped. "And what did they find?"

"Nothing major. But there are some calls to London. We've a bad feeling that she's going to hit one of the museums there."

"Dammit," Matt said. This was turning into a quagmire before his eyes. "Is Coyote on his way there?"

"He'll be landing in an hour."

"But that's it? London?"

"That's all."

"What a mess. I'll make some calls then," said Matt. He remembered the listening device below his desk and wondered if he should tell Tim.

Tim brushed his blond long hair to one side and smiled. "Very well. Tell me what you need next. All right?"

Matt smiled back. Tim always reminded him of a surfer and never seemed to belong to this company.

"You all right?" Tim asked, screwing up his blue eyes.

"I'm fine," Matt said, rubbing his temples.

"You sure? You seem rough. Especially since this mission started," Tim said. He ran his hand through his hair. "I've also been think—"

Matt shook his head and placed his finger on his lips.

Tim cocked his head and it took a second before he understood. He nodded.

"It's a tough job is what I mean," Tim said.

"It is. But we signed up for it," Matt said. He scribbled something on his paper and Tim nodded.

"Call me when you need anything," Tim said as he left the office. "Oh, and you have a visitor."

Matt stood up to stretch out his back. The intercom buzzed and he pressed it.

"You have a meeting," said Jimmy, his assistant.

"Christ. I thought I didn't have any today."

"It's a walk-in sir."

"A walk-in? Well tell them to make an appointment for another time. I'm busy."

"I think you should take it."

"What?" Matt had never known Jimmy to contradict him.

"It's Interpol," whispered Jimmy.

Matt's other phone started to ring. It was his boss. "Send her in," Matt said without thinking.

He picked up the phone.

"Great mission, isn't it?"

Matt was certain that his boss was only now watching the thermal images.

"It's something else." In his periphery he could see the door open and a small figure step into his room. He swiveled his chair and faced his window. From this angle all he could see was the building across the avenue.

"How did the conference go?"

"As expected," said Matt. "They want full system backing for the mission. I said fine."

"Good. Good. The Texan seem a little antsy?"

"He did. But someone just stole something from him. That's to be expected."

"All right. So get the woman and all this will be settled."

"I will," Matt said. He wondered why his boss would call to say something so asinine. It wasn't like him to micromanage. Or call for a silly update he already knew. Perhaps he too was feeling the fire from the oligarchs.

"I heard you have a visitor from Interpol."

"I do," said Matt. His brain lurched. Could it be that his boss was the one who planted the listening device? But why?

"Let me know how it goes. Don't give any information away."

"Bu—"

"You heard me. If they give us problems let me know. The Texan knows enough people who can squeeze them back if they cause problems."

"All right. And about the next city," Matt said. Everything about this mission stunk. He reminded himself to be extra careful and to make sure he wasn't the fall man.

"Don't tell them that, for Christ sakes."

"We'll have to let State know."

"No we don't… Get to me first before you go bull horning this. This isn't like other missions. All right?"

"Right," said Matt. He looked up and his phone slipped

from his hands. Catching it, he controlled the tremors that pulsated through his body and placed the receiver down with both hands.

"Nervous?" the woman asked. Her smile wasn't nervous. This time, it was confident. Almost as if she was ready to eat him up.

"Jay. How nice to see you again. You look different," Matt said. He could feel a rush of blood to his skin as his heart bounced about near his neck.

"Imports, huh?" she said, pointing at his desk and him.

She had on a smart dress and blouse, gray, with her hair tied in a bonnet. With her confidence she looked at least five years older. Matt found himself staring away from her eyes and looked down at his desk.

"I'm sorry, but I can't discuss go right now," he finally said, surprised that his mind came up with anything for it seemed bereft of words.

She leaned back and laughed. Matt relaxed.

"I'm not here to discuss go, Matt." Jay walked up to him and pulled out her badge. Matt felt himself shrivel up.

"*You're* Interpol?" he asked.

"That's right."

He examined the badge. It was legitimate. "And your name's Kim."

"That's right."

"You lied," he said, feeling her eyes pierce through him.

"Mr. Imports will now lecture me on all the bad things about lying?"

"You lied twice," he replied. "You said you were a student."

"Oh, but I am."

"A student of life?" he said.

She smiled and pointed at him. He wasn't certain what that meant, but he couldn't help grinning. He took in a few deep breaths, feeling too self-aware for his own tastes.

"May I ask what you're here for?"

"I think you know what I'm here for," she said.

It was moments like these when Matt really wished he kept a flask of whiskey on him. He rubbed his temples.

"Bad day?" she asked.

He wasn't certain if she was mocking him. He remembered where he was, and he knew he needed to act tougher. He looked into her eyes. He could feel the room shrinking.

"Please tell me your business here," he said. He could feel his voice turn into a growl.

She tilted her head a small fraction of a degree. "Oh? Okay. Do you want to tell me what happened in Crete last night?"

"I'm not sure, what happened?"

She pointed her finger at him again, as if she wanted to poke his eye out. "Don't play dumb with me. Or else I'll start pulling out subpoenas for all the international laws your company just violated."

Matt raised his eyebrows. "Really? And just how are you going to manage that? You do understand who owns this company, don't you?"

"It doesn't matter. You're a private company. If you violate international law there's nothing that can protect you."

Matt scoffed. "Do you even understand how the world works?" he said. "You should stick to go."

Her cocky demeanor immediately melted, and she shrunk back. Matt immediately regretted being so harsh. But he didn't say anything to comfort her. He just couldn't know what her real intentions were. Interpol was a powerful organization, and he didn't need them breathing down his neck.

"You're not invincible and you're not protected," she said. Her voice almost cracked.

"Yes we are," said Matt. He could feel the tension crackling in the room. "But let's not argue. What's the problem in Crete?"

Kim seemed to consider his olive branch and looked down at her hands. She wanted to say something. Matt knew that the listening device was recording every part of their conversation. He couldn't, however, let Kim know that.

"Let's not," she finally said.

"I'm going to head out for lunch in an hour. How about you join me?" he asked.

She nodded. "In the cafe two blocks north of here. You know it?" she said.

"My favorite place," he said.

An hour later Matt stepped out of the building. The sun peeked out from behind dark grey clouds. The edges sparkled before more clouds snuffed out the sun. A breeze picked up, and Matt wrapped his scarf on tighter.

He walked north, the honking and hum of engines didn't penetrate his thoughts. He felt an oppressive weight on his head. The Coyote would soon be in London and he'd get to finding that woman. And he'd kill her. Meanwhile here, Matt was going to have to deal with Interpol. He'd managed to bluff Kim into backing down, but the truth was Interpol *could* severely hamper the company. And if they did that, Matt would be a pawn that the company would use to solve its problem.

He'd just got off the phone with his parents. They were in low spirits as the house was falling apart. His father was too old to fix anything, and the neighbors, living in a town that had just lost a car factory, had too many problems of their own to help them. Talking to his parents always reminded him that he needed his job more than ever.

He turned a corner, a man was handing out pamphlets. Matt moved to avoid the man, but the man gave a slight whistle and a nod at his other hand. Matt took the pamphlet. He looked at it. An advertisement to redeem gold. A piece of paper flapped from the inside. Matt pulled it out. "Walk past the cafe. On next street turn right."

He walked past the cafe, not looking inside. Was this a joke? He was certain it had to be Kim. He reminded himself that she could very well be trying to throw him off balance.

He turned the corner, and he felt a pinch on his elbow.

"Don't look at me, just walk."

His arm curled reflexively, but he didn't fight back. She'd a hold of his funny bone. She pushed him into the back of a waiting limo, it's back door already open.

"The FDR," she said. The limo driver took off. Matt could smell old leather and sweat. Kim, sitting next to him, smiled. "You were being followed," she said.

Matt indicated that the driver could hear them.

"That's okay," she said. "He's with us."

Matt wondered if "us" included him. He felt hot, so he tried not to look at her for too long. He glanced behind him, and he saw a man in a trench coat turn the corner and look around. He didn't recognize the man, but Matt knew when someone was a tail. A cascade of thoughts hit his mind.

"You were keeping an eye on me?" Matt said.

"Of course. How else am I supposed to ascertain a safe meeting?"

The limo merged into a freeway and immediately stopped.

"Rush hour," said Matt softly. "Who was that?"

"I don't know. You know you're getting into some messy business, don't you?"

"My company's business *is* messy business."

"But sending The Coyote to kill an old man and burn down his house? You don't think that's going too far?"

"It's not the first time," Matt said. He wondered why someone from Interpol was acting like such a girl scout. She sounded smart, so he decided that she was still playing games.

"Well, it's the last time then. At least if I've anything to do with it."

"You know my bosses?"

"I do. And I know how well connected they are, and how many strings they pulled to get access to an observational drone for last night's mission. I know all that." She huffed and looked out her window.

She seemed defeated, vulnerable, and Matt placed a hand on her shoulder.

"How can you work for such people?" she asked, her eyes narrowing.

"I need the money. Not like there're any better choices in today's world. The people who control your organization are much the same as my bosses—"

"This Texan oil-man," she said, her words tinged with disgust.

"That's right. He knows enough Senators and members of the EU that he doesn't need to worry."

"We too were following the old man," said Kim.

"Oh? Were you building a case?"

"We didn't have much," said Kim. "But he was ruffling feathers in Europe as well."

"He and his accomplice were playing that sort of game… in the end you're doing what I'm doing."

She glared at him. He removed his hand from her shoulder.

"I'm just saying," Matt continued, "that we're both tools for evil men."

"*We* don't kill men for nothing."

"Yes you do," said Matt. He didn't like where this conversation was turning; he felt out of his depth. "You kill their spirits."

She rolled her eyes. "Are you saying that legal systems are the same as blood-feuds?" She shook her head. "You Americans are all alike… I'm not here to argue with you about the pillars of civilization. I thought we could come to some sort of mutual agreement," she said.

"Fine. We sent Coyote to kill the old man. The Texan wanted blood, what can I say?"

"The old man stole from him then? So why not tell us? That's the best way to get an APB for a stolen piece of art. This way he might never find it."

Matt screwed his face at Kim. "How much do you know about the old man and his busy bee?"

"That they're thieves. Why else are you after them?"

"My *company* is after them," said Matt, holding up a finger. "But they're no ordinary thieves. From what we know they're out to correct past ills."

"Who do they work for?"

"No one that I can see. But my bosses have plenty of illegal artifacts that they would rather just hold on to."

"Like?" Kim asked.

"Artifacts from the Baghdad Museum. They were some of the ones who paid people to rob the place. So he wanted to keep everything hush hush."

"But these two have robbed from others too."

"What did they steal?"

"Egyptian Art in France, even some Indian Art from the Iranians," she said with a certain glee. Matt hoped she felt the same as he did.

"You don't see the similarities?" Matt asked.

She shook her head. He liked her mannerisms. Almost every movement of hers tricked his blood into moving faster. He reminded himself to remain professional.

"All the things they've stolen have been stolen in the past. They're just here to correct wrongs."

"Two wrongs don't make a right," she said.

Her comment was too instinctive for his tastes. He moved away from her. "How can you care about the rights of thieves?" He turned and stared at the window. They were moving now, past the flat boardwalk on the Hudson. He could smell her rose infused perfume. He tried to think of something else.

"There's more to you than meets the eye," she said. She placed her hand on his. "Whose side are you on?"

"The right one. But that doesn't matter, I'm here to do a job." He wasn't certain what he meant.

"I know. As am I," she said and squeezed his hand. "And you will let Coyote into London to do what he wants?"

An image of the old man on his knees rushed across Matt's mind. "He's only good for one thing, and that's killing. He can't gather intel for the life of him. I'll go to London."

"Will you make sure that he doesn't do the same thing he did in Crete?" Kim asked.

Matt thought about what she said for a second. Was that all she wanted? Some damage control so no one complained? If Coyote had weighted and dropped the old man's body in the sea she wouldn't have cared, would she? Matt looked her over. He knew what had to be done, and he knew he'd have to use her.

"I'll make sure of that. But you need to keep me informed of anything you learn," he said.

"I will, as long as you do." She seemed to have sensed his change of demeanor and backed away from him.

"And I'll need access to your assets."

She thought this over for a second. "All right. But you need to tell me if you find out when and where she's striking."

"I will," said Matt. The limo was pulling up around 125th. "I'll get off here."

"Are you sure? It's uptown."

"I can get back."

The limo came to halt. Some cars behind honked. Matt stepped out. He felt Kim's hand squeeze his. A piece of paper slid into his pocket.

"My number," she said, with a smile.

He gave a terse okay.

"You're hatching something up, aren't you?" she said,

cocking her head.

"No." He didn't like it that his voice was low. It was always low when he lied.

"Whose side are you on?" she asked again.

"The right one," Matt said and walked towards the subway station.

"You from here?" the man with hairy knuckles asked.

"No," said Coral. She shifted away so that the man could see she wasn't interested. Her mind was focused on seeing her father. As she debarked from the plane, losing the hairy man, she could feel her muscles trembling. She put it off to dehydration from the plane ride, but she knew better. She climbed into a car in the parking lot. It was an old Fiat. The engine redone. By father.

She drove out of the parking lot. Her breaths grew shallow, and she forced herself to breathe deep. A car cut her off. She yelled and honked her horn. She knew this wasn't the way. She wouldn't make the hour long drive if she was this on edge. She waved at the driver and blew the cutting offender a kiss.

But her body wouldn't listen that easily. It trembled like it knew something was wrong. She didn't believe in the supernatural and so tried to remind herself that she was simply overreacting to father not calling back.

She blared some trance music on the radio, and it helped a little. Soon she was driving down a winding road, the smell of the sea calming her down more than her thoughts ever could. And as she was about to turn onto the street she'd known all her life, anticipating this last mile to be a walk down memory lane, she noticed a man standing on the corner. He wasn't doing anything. But the way his eyes graced her car, she knew *something* was wrong. She drove straight instead of turning.

A mile later, in the midst of a small forest, the smell of cones and olive tree leaves strong in the air, she parked out of sight from the road and waited. Her heart beat fast and her hands shook. A few cars drove by. None of them seemed to be especially innocuous. But she couldn't be sure. She walked through the forest, away from all the trails. Every five minutes she'd stop and listen, hoping to hear, through the chirps of the birds and buzz of insects, something that would tip her off that another person was here. It took her several minutes before she came close to her house. She remembered playing in these forests, and when she was old enough, her father telling her that she'd have to learn them and know when someone was here when they didn't belong.

On her belly, she slid to an outcrop of rocks. She could hear a few voices. They were gruff, strange. She didn't like violence, but she knew she should've brought a gun. She could smell ashes of cement and wood in the air. Steadying herself, she peered over a rock.

Her heart stopped and caved in. The house she grew up in had been burned to the ground. She stared at it. A couple of policemen were outside, sifting through it. But there were also some men who didn't seem like policemen. And they didn't seem Greek. A few dogs appeared from the wreckage. She was upwind, so she was safe. Just then, the wind started to shift. There was no way she could be caught here. But she had to find out what happened. She knew of only one person.

She slid back from the rocks, back into the forest. The wind shifted and the dogs started to bark. She heard boots crunching on rocks. Fast. She ran. After a second she dived behind a bush. The dogs appeared around the rocks. She held her breath. She had no gun. What was she going to do? She couldn't outrun them, they would only cut her off by the roads, encircle her, and capture her. The men, the non-Greeks, appeared and sifted through the rocks. The dogs were fighting over something. The men shook their heads.

Coral sighed in relief when she saw them turn and disappear, pulling the dogs with them.

She backed away slowly and made her way to the car. But the car didn't seem the same as she left it. She stared at it from a hundred meters away trying to think of what seemed so different? Her guts rumbled. Was she just getting nervous? That didn't matter, especially if her guts were right about father.

The place she knew was a small town on the edge of Crete. Twenty miles away. She broke out in a slow trot.

By midnight she was staring at the small town. Her skin was tight from dried sweat, her throat, parched, and her eyelids felt heavy. She shifted, her muscles were turning into knots from the long run. Her legs moaned. But she had to see if father's friend was there.

The town was half asleep. A few people walked the streets, and the bar that the friend owned had a few patrons sitting around, chatting. She couldn't see who it was. But she wasn't ready to walk out into the well-lit streets.

A few yells from drunks sounded out, and she jumped. She didn't like this, this feeling weak. She walked to a dark building facing the rocks and forest and entered the town. For all she knew, this could be a trap. She swiveled her head at the slightest noise.

A few dogs barked as she walked by, but no one stirred to their chorus.

Finally, she found herself on the edge of a well-lit street, across from the bar. She could see her father's friend talking to a few men. The men seemed like the typical Greek male in this free falling economy: young with nothing to do. She watched to see if there were any characteristics that would make them seem out of place. Her heart rose to her throat. She was extremely wary of getting caught. Everything seemed too perfect, too easy. The smell of her charred childhood home came back to her.

A few more patrons left the bar. The friend bid them good-bye. She wondered how many of the jobless men would've been willing to turn her in for a few extra Euro. Everyone was a potential eye for the powerful here. That's what times like these caused.

And again the charred smell came back to her. She wondered if her father's body was underneath that rubble. Or perhaps it was in a morgue somewhere waiting for a proper autopsy report. The smoke probably killed him, or knocked him unconscious and a beam came crashing down after that. *Or perhaps something else happened.* She pictured her Father dead before the fire started. Why were those men there? Those dogs? What did the non-Greeks want?

A shriek of pain stopped the thoughts. She massaged her temples.

The last two men left, and she watched as her father's friend cleaned up. She waited until the tight feeling in her head subsided, and she could coax her body forward. She walked as calmly as she could across the street. The friend, wiping a few tables looked up.

"Coral?" he whispered when she was a few feet away.

She nodded her heard, no words coming out of her mouth though she wanted to speak.

"Come in," he said and ushered her in. He shut the door, locked it.

"What are you doing here?" he asked.

She wanted to say something, but felt her head spinning too fast. She sat down on a stool.

"Oh Coral," he said and walked up to her. He grabbed a glass of water and handed it to her. "Drink up," he said.

"What happened, Alexandros?" she asked.

He stared at her for a second. "You don't know?"

"I just came back into town. I hadn't heard from him…" She sipped the water. It tasted funny, like chemicals almost. She could smell Alexandros' cologne, sweat, beer, and cigarettes all mixed with the bleach-washcloth that stood nearby. That grounded her, and she looked into Alexandros' blue eyes. She forgot how striking they were. He claimed heritage from the Vikings, though she wasn't sure when the Vikings ever swung this far south. As a child she'd always look to him for advice when father wasn't there. Now, he was getting old, his movements slower, the bags and wrinkles around his eyes more pronounced.

"I saw the burned house," she said.

"I know. They took me in to identify the body."

Her heart dropped. "The police?" she said through a tight throat.

"Of course," he said. "They said it was murder and arson."

"Oh," she said. She somehow expected that. "How?"

"Execution," he said, pointing his forefinger at his head.

She could smell his beer breath now that he'd moved closer. "Were there any men there that didn't belong?" she asked. She was trying her hardest to be stolid.

His blue eyes danced back and forth on her face. "It's okay to show some weakness, Coral," he said. "We always worried about you. That you were trying to be too tough. For all the women in the world. For... For whatever reason." He placed his hand on hers.

A memory, of Alexandros and her father smiling at her and kissing her goodbye as she went on her first solo journey through Europe, hit her. She blinked, and felt a sting in her eyes. Her body uncontrollably shivered and tears trickled down her face.

Alexandros hugged her. He patted her back and squeezed. It took a minute before she pulled away. He handed her a handkerchief.

She blew out her nose. It had really happened.

"A drink?" he said, reaching over for a bottle of wine.

"No. I need to be clear-headed," she replied.

"You can prepare for war tomorrow. Today, relax." He pointed his finger in the sky. "And drink to his memory, to his loving eyes watching down on us... Oh sorry. To his memory," he said nodding at her. He knew she didn't believe.

"That's okay. To his eyes," she said, because she would rather feel his eyes on her than not, and she *could* feel them.

Alexandros opened the bottle and poured out two glasses.

They toasted, and she drank. He placed his glass down.

"There were men there who weren't Greek," he said.

"What did they look like?" She felt a tickle on her skin, as if something about him was amiss.

"Two men. Bigger than they needed to be. Square jaws. Dark brown hair. I think I heard American accents, but I'm not sure."

"I saw men like that at the house," she said. "They had dogs."

He shrugged. "They could be helping the local police," he said.

"They didn't ask you anything?"

"No. Just asked me to identify. I told them we were old friends who fell out. I didn't mention you," he said.

She paused. "So what do you think?"

He took in a handful of loud breaths, while reaching over for his glass and drinking the rest of the wine. "What do I know? You father never told me what he was up to. That was one of the reasons I left. And I never bothered him about what he did. I always loved him. Always will. But what he did... And I'm sure what you did, is not for me to judge. But am I right in guessing it might be the reason for this... end?"

She didn't know what to say. There was some anger at how he so quickly blamed their occupation on what happened. But then, he was almost certainly right. So she suppressed that initial anger. Besides, she wanted to hear more from this man who knew her father more intimately and for a longer period than she ever did.

"Is *that* why you left?" she asked. She remembered when he moved out one day. Preceded by days of tumultuous fighting and yelling. Both men had low voices, so the fight, in her child's ears, sounded like the roaring of boars. It was followed by a long time without seeing him. Then he started to visit again. The love between the men was palpable, it was obvious in those few pauses, or glances, but it had cooled from what it once was.

"It was partially the reason. He was hard to live with, and in the end, as much as it hurt me, I knew I had to leave."

"But you loved each other, why not work through it?"

"I could have," he said and poured himself another glass. "But, then he always loved you more."

She sipped her wine, then drank the rest of it. Could it be that Alexandros was jealous of a father's love? She didn't know what to say. He placed his hand on her shoulder. "It wasn't you. Don't think about it for a second. I had to leave. But I knew that he had your love, and that he would remain happy."

She wasn't sure what he meant, so she let him pour her another drink.

"I need to get the police files on the case."

"I can get them," he said.

"I don't—"

"Come on, Coral. I'm an old man. And if these bastards— whatever you've done to them—have dared to kill my lover, then the least I can do is spend the remaining years of my life helping you out."

She smiled, felt tears bubbling up. "Thank you."

"Of course."

They drank a few more glasses, as he played a small radio with old Greek tunes.

"He used to love this music," Alexandros said and rocked his head to the beat.

"I know," she said. "I always asked him to switch it off." She remembered being a teenager and playing Nirvana as loud as she could to get him to shut his music off. Suddenly, she felt disgusted with herself for having been such a handful.

"I know," Alexandros said laughing. "He complained when you became a teenager, but I reminded him what a good girl you were."

"Tell me the story of how he found me," she asked.

Alexandros paused, grew serious, and shifted in his chair. A car drove by. "Did he ever tell you?" he asked.

"Never specifics. He always said that I was a gift from God."

"Nothing else?"

Coral shook her head. She remembered how they fought over this issue. How he never wanted to tell her the whole story.

"Well, I met him when he was eighteen. I was sixteen, away from home and doing work," Alexandros said and pulled out a pack of cigarettes. He offered Coral one, but she refused.

"Back then I was confused, so we were only friends. I think he knew, but I didn't. I found work with a fisherman here near town, and I was working long hours. Your father was writer back then—"

"He wrote?"

"He fancied himself a better version of Dostoevsky," Alexandros said while puffing on a cigarette.

Coral smiled. She'd only ever seen Father write in his journal.

"He lived with a girl. He wasn't doing anything with her, just letting her stay with him. But of course, the town's rumors were rich. They were certain this writer man was doing all sorts of sick things with an underage girl. Your father ignored it all."

Another car drove by. It seemed to be faster than normal. That forced Coral to look around, as if someone could have snuck in without her noticing.

"And one day she got pregnant. I wasn't sure how, your father wasn't either. The girl was running around with some rough men near the bars, so it was only a matter of time…" Alexandros said. He thought for a second. He seemed to be weighing something in his head.

"The girl was disgraced, she didn't know what to do. You

73

have to remember the time. It was still very conservative back then. And it turns out that her family was the next town over. And news travels fast." Alexandros took another drag of his cigarette.

"But your father was such gallant man. He took it upon himself to tell everyone it was his child. The girl, of course, was thankful. She could hide behind him. And she did."

The pause this time, with Alexandros looking off into the wall behind Coral, felt final.

"But what about the girl?" she asked.

"She gave birth. Then she disappeared. Some said she was running with some smugglers, and they got tired of her and dumped her. Who knows? Her family had the police looking everywhere. But in the end it was just another poor girl lost in the world. No country stops for that."

"That was my mother," Coral said, though she already knew the answer.

Alexandros nodded and blew out smoke. "You were always his daughter," he said.

He started to cough. She took the cigarette out of his mouth and led him upstairs to the room above the bar. His eyes were glazed, and he seemed not to know she was there anymore. She tucked him into bed. It was funny, only a few decades ago she could remember him tucking her into bed. She slept on the floor beside him, listening to the road for anything out of place, and thinking about her father.

The next morning, after Alexandros cooked his famous eggs, Coral waited as he went out to the police station. From a crack in the second story window, she watched the streets. Nothing was amiss. And she watched as Alexandros hobbled back home. No one was following him. She relaxed a little.

"Photocopies."

Coral nodded and sifted through the papers he'd brought her.

"H—"

"There wasn't anyone out of place. And the police knew about me and your father. It wasn't hard."

"They didn't find anything in the house," she said.

"Cleaned out, most likely," he said.

She wondered how he would know that, but she kept quiet and read. There wasn't anything new. The police found an exit wound consistent with an execution. They weren't sure who could have done such a thing. None of the neighbors or friends knew of any enemies. They were looking for a young woman who was known to live with him. She might have been a lover and this might be a lover's quarrel.

"The police are still no good, are they?" she said.

Alexandros chuckled. "They don't paid enough, what do you expect?"

"There's nothing to go off here," she said.

"There's something," he said and pointed out a page.

She read it. Neighbors had seen a car drive by on the night of the murder. A figure had snuck to the house, in the dark. No one was sure what happened next. Possibly a scream. But then all was quiet and the figure left. A woman who lived a house over was outside staring at the stars, said the figure moved like a coyote. This witness cannot be collaborated, and she admitted to smoking marijuana while this was going on.

Coral shook her head. "What does that even mean?"

"That the it was most likely a man and that he was trained. That's what moving like a coyote means. A coyote moves to its next meal, nothing more, nothing less."

"But the person who saw this was high," she replied.

"Coral," Alexandros said, shaking his head. "You've never been high, have you?"

She shook her head. She'd seen some of her school friends get high and knew it wasn't for her. And she knew how worthless they'd have been as witnesses.

"When someone's high they're still valid witnesses."

"She said she saw a coyote. Could it be that she was hallucinating?"

"Few people hallucinate when high," he said. "Wait." He walked off to a closet of his and pulled out a clear plastic bag. He sat back down in front of her. When he opened the bag she was hit by the strong pungent smell of weed. She hadn't smelled that since she left school. She sneered.

"This helps me a lot," he said. And grinned. He pulled out a paper and threw some of the green leaves onto it. He rolled the paper over the substance in both hands, and with his thumbs rolled it into a cylinder. He pulled out a lighter and handed it to her.

"I'm not," she said with both hands raised in the air.

"This is part of your experiment," he said. "So you know that this witness isn't crazy."

She placed the joint in her mouth and lit it up.

"Inhale, deeper. Hold it," he said.

She did as he said and the smoke, unlike cigarette smoke, felt softer, almost like a friend entering her and then settled in her lungs like a rock. And from there it grew, warmth spreading through her body, her extremities, her head. And it exploded up her throat. She coughed it all up. After a few minutes of coughing, and Alexandros laughing, she recovered.

"I don't feel anything," she said.

Alexandros, puffing away at what remained, grinned and opened the window. "No? I always thought I bought the best hash in town…"

A breeze flew in from the window. She felt it on her skin. Then it lingered on her skin and a tingle ran through her. She smiled. There was warmth all over her body, like a fire inside, and it met the cool on her skin, and she leaned back and laughed.

Alexandros laughed. He had a video camera out.

"Someone cannot be a witness on this," Coral said, laughing. The spell subsided and she saw he was looking out the window. She walked up to him.

"What is it?"

"Describe what you see," he said.

She stared at the street, a good feeling all swishing about in her head. Her mind was going places she couldn't choose and it suddenly focused in on movement everywhere on the street. "I see an empty street. But I also see a man with a cane walking. His left foot troubles him. He's taking his time, so I know he has nowhere to be. There's a fly on his shoulder. It seems to have found a home. Oh, and there's a bird," she said, looking to the sky. "It's free, like I want to be, and it's looking down upon all of us. Free—"

"All right," Alexandros said, switching off his video camera. "That's enough." He had a smile on his face. "Let's go eat some food."

"I'm not hungry," she said.

"But you will be."

Alexandros spent an hour cooking up food, while she ate off the bowls he was using. She felt herself being more of a nuisance than she normally was, but she didn't care, and Alexandros' smile only encouraged her.

The meal consisted of two fish and a rice pilaf that she remembered from her childhood. She finished it all. Her belly bursting, she still wanted more.

And she collapsed into a fitful sleep.

"Wake up."

She awoke, Alexandros' face smiling above her. Her head felt as clear as it had ever been.

"What time is it?" she asked.

"Four. You slept for a little bit," he said. "And you ate all my food." He smiled.

He helped her up.

Sitting up made her realize that some remnants of the weed still floated in her head. She smiled. Thoughts were floating around in her head faster than she could deal with them.

"You never told me where you disappeared to," she said. "When you left us." She didn't mean for it to come out like that, but Alexandros didn't seem to take it badly.

"I never mentioned it. But that was a big part of our fight. Like I said it wasn't you. I was also going into the service..."

"Military?" she asked because he just didn't seem like the type.

"No. Intel. I'm of French background."

"And how long?"

"Ten years before I got tired of it. That was a big thing for your father. That I was willing to sleep with a government, any government, made him sick."

"And..." she wanted so badly to tell him what they were doing.

"And that also means that I've friends in Interpol and other places that will help us get more answers than our police friends here will."

"Do you know what we did?" she asked. "Do you want to know?"

He closed his eyes. A moist line formed on them. "I know how he was," he said. "There's no need for me to know more."

"Well, I'm running out of ideas," she said.

"Let's go back to basics. The police report." He pulled out his video camera.

"Oh no. Did you record my stupidity?"

"Some," he said, and pressed play.

She saw the scene on the street. Her voice came over. It sounded more masculine than she liked. But what mattered was that she described the scene accurately.

"See?" he said as he switched off the video.

"So the woman was a valuable witness."

"She saw things a normal person might have glossed over. Remember that."

"All right."

"So we know we're up against a professional. What else do we know?"

"The police report had nothing else."

"True. Who would be angry enough to want to kill you?"

"Many people," she said.

"Then who can pay someone to come at you?"

She thought it out. She didn't like having the secret of Alexandros not knowing.

"Write it down," he said.

"I have to tell you then."

"I don't have to see."

Her eyes went over his wrinkled face, his kind face. "We robbed from many powerful people," she said.

He didn't seem surprised. "He was always about righting wrongs. I told him he was fool for thinking like that."

"I think the same way too," she said.

He smiled. "Of course you do."

That sounded patronizing and once again she wondered why he was helping her, and her paranoia spiked, and she wondered if perhaps he was luring her into a trap to incriminate herself.

"Don't get paranoid," he said. "The weed will do that."

She giggled.

"What were the last few robberies?"

She explained the robbery in Manhattan. She explained the ones before that: from museums with private showings and those from mansions in various locales.

"You resell all these?"

She shook her head. "Only to get some money to live. We meant this to be a way to correct old wrongs. People in the places that were robbed were more than happy to receive these items back."

Alexandros nodded. "Fair enough. But there are two people who might be after you. The Texan with the oil. I've heard of him before; he has a lot of power in Washington and he has stakes in a private intel company. And if you stole from Tehran, there's no telling what *they'll* do," he said shaking his head. "You're a crazy one."

She felt tired again, and hungry.

"Let me ask questions. But you'll have to leave."

They exchanged information, and adopted words to help them identify if the other was in trouble, and if a line was no longer secure—"nothing but love"—to be spoken on the first sentence. He asked her where else she could stay, and she said London was still fine; the flat was paid for until the end of the year.

"Just don't go robbing again," he said.

She didn't promise. When she hugged him she held him tight, smelling his sweat and old clothes. She wished then that she could live a normal life, perhaps be a waitress here with him, but she knew that she was beyond the point of no return.

He gave her two new phones. Phone cards. And some websites to leave messages.

That night, when he drove her to the airport, her head was abuzz with questions for him, but instead of asking, she stared at the buildings and trees that flashed by.

At the airport she leaned in for a kiss. They embraced.

"Are you smoking for a reason?" she asked, the question having just popped into her head.

He looked ahead. A policeman was telling cars to not stop for too long.

"I have cancer. A couple years, the doctors say," he said.

"Painful?" she asked, wondering what sort of person she was to be leaving him.

"Not as painful as losing..." He looked down at his hands. "You should get going."

She wasn't certain if he meant it. She didn't want to leave the only other attachment in her life. Her past was her future, or so she'd always believed.

"Do you have someone, Coral?" he asked as a plane screamed overhead.

"No," she said, thinking about Drake.

"I know you're smart and tough. And you don't need someone. But you do. Life is nothing to go through without someone to love."

"I loved father. You."

"But…" he said then sighed.

Her heart throbbed with a sharp pain. She didn't want to leave.

"Go," he said. "And we'll toast again in a few months."

She fought back the tears in her eyes and hugged him again.

"You'll be fine," he said. "You're tough. I'm proud of you. And your father was always proud of you."

She darted into the airport, telling herself that she wouldn't look back.

Back in London, rain misting down, she sat in her flat eating English food. When the feeling in her chest grew too strong, she called Drake. He invited her over.

Matt bought the plane tickets after talking to Kim. He wondered how many laws he'd violated by not reporting to his bosses what his plans were. He packed a light suitcase and called for a taxi. He had to make a stop by the office.

"Any news Tim?" he asked through his office phone.

"No. Not yet. Coyote's in London. I think you're to have a conference in a few hours."

"No time," Matt said. "I'm heading over to London right this moment."

"What? Do they know you're going?"

Matt assumed they would, with the listening device in his office. "That Crete job was messed up. I'm here to make sure that London doesn't get botched up too. Call me with any updates."

"Oh, we've gone through everything. We even have his phone records," Tim said. He was chewing on something again. "Everything comes up empty. He's good, whoever he was."

"Nothing else on his life?"

"Nope. People in the town, cops included, are pretty tight lipped."

"I thought we'd have some boys down there."

"They claim to have a friend there, but he was a dead end."

Matt stopped himself from barking orders and having that friend watched.

"Well," he said. "That's what happens when you send a nut job to do the work of a professional."

Tim laughed. "Will you tell him that when you see him in London?"

"This is London. We can't go pissing off MI5."

A long pause from Tim made Matt wonder if he'd gone too far.

"Well, we have the CIA in the palm of our hands, so why not MI5? Besides, didn't you hear?"

"What?" asked Matt.

"The Texan pulled some strings over at State. Now the old man and the woman, whoever she is, are on the terrorist watch list as of an hour ago."

"How—"

"Come on Matt, this isn't your first rodeo, is it? We sent evidence to the CIA, who verified it, and now we can do whatever we want to the woman. So Coyote's going to be fine."

"Good, good," he forced himself to say. He knew that Tim wasn't stupid enough to mention that the evidence was fabricated. Or that in the CIA they had agents who worked for the company as well, and who would sign off on anything they sent over.

"Well, gotta go," Matt said.

"You're still going to head over?" Tim asked.

Matt knew that it was always better to beg for forgiveness than to ask for permission. "Send me information when you get it," he said again.

"Of course."

"One more thing, where's the Coyote staying?"

Tim mouthed off the hotel, though there was no room.

Matt hung up and headed out.

He landed in Heathrow and took a taxi in. The streets were empty at this time of night, and he felt like he'd rather be near people. He checked into the same hotel as Coyote. It was near London Bridge.

A knock sounded on his door. He wondered if he'd ordered anything.

He opened it and felt the weight of the door push back on him. Shifting his weight, he used his arm to throw the door back and get a look at his assailant. It was a man in a hoodie. A silenced pistol pointed at him. Matt froze. The man walked in. Matt couldn't see his face.

"What the hell do *you* want?" the man growled as he

83

closed the door behind him.

"Coyote?" Matt asked. He knew the voice. It was full of youthful vigor, yet low and grating, like he'd been smoking cigarettes for too long.

The man took off his hoodie. He had a bent nose, and scars all over his hands and face. He grinned. His shiny white teeth blinding Matt.

"Christ," Matt said and sat down on a chair. "Some fucking entrance."

"I scare you?" Coyote asked. There was no humor in his voice.

"You scare nothing," Matt replied, though he could feel his heart racing. He knew that Coyote was crazy enough to do anything. It was best not to show fear. Matt nodded at the mini-fridge. "Get yourself a whiskey."

"I know you watched me in Crete," said Coyote.

Matt looked over at Coyote, who didn't waver with his stare. Matt didn't put it past the assassin to have placed that listening device in his office.

"I'm in charge here," Matt said and lumbered over to the mini-fridge. "Johnny Walker's fine with you?"

Coyote continued to hold his grim stare, then sat down. "Sure, that's fine."

Matt poured two fingers into two plastic cups. The smell of the stout malt made his mouth water and his mind anticipate the hit of alcohol. He wanted to see how on edge Coyote was, so he poured the cups so that his body blocked the view. He walked over to Coyote with one hand extended. Coyote reached in and grabbed the one further away. Matt held tight for a second, felt Coyote pull harder and released. Matt stared at his cup, then grinned at Coyote.

Matt raised his cup and they both bumped cups, the plastic letting out a hollow sound.

Matt sipped his after pausing for a second before Coyote sipped his too. Matt held the liquor in his mouth for a second, feeling the sting and open of his taste buds, and he let the liquid drop into his throat. He'd always fought hard to stay away from alcohol. Stories of an uncle who was much like him and died of liver failure haunted him. But as he grew older he wondered why he fought his nature so much, and wondered why he took up a job where he would drink across from an assassin.

"You're still the same," Coyote said. The muscles under the left side of his nose snarled up. "You feint with great precision, but that's all you ever were: someone who faked it. No wonder you left the field for the office.

"I'm still in charge," Matt said. He hoped it didn't sound as hollow to Coyote as it did to him.

"Oh really? Then why are your bosses hiring me against your wishes? Why did you watch me on a mission that isn't yours?"

"You want me to cut funds?" Matt said and watched with some pleasure as Coyote's flinched. "Then you'll report to me. We're in England now, and we can't have you acting like an idiot."

Of course, it'd been a long time since Matt had trained Coyote with all the field knowledge he had. A long time before seeing his student surpass him in skill, know it, and take off on his own. Matt knew he'd to be careful because Coyote did indeed have the backing of his bosses. And, in the end, Matt knew the assassin was no longer the loner who named himself Coyote and was happy with the Tier-One missions he'd been given. Now he was older and clever enough to find a network, like the Texan-magnate, to support his habit of killing.

"I'm the best you have, and I know you tried to cast me out, but you couldn't, could you?" Coyote said and finished his drink. He held his cup out, tapping the edge.

Matt leaned for the whiskey and swung the bottle over to Coyote's cup.

Matt didn't remember him drinking more than one, and that was usually to save real estate at a bar before a hit.

"Say when," Matt said as he poured, suddenly feeling fatherly towards the man in front of him.

"That's good," Coyote said and pulled back the cup. His voice had softened.

"And what are you doing here, Matt? I *know* they didn't say you could interfere."

"That's what the old goat told you?"

"Lots of old goats tell me that. I'm their goto guy, and it's for a reason."

"Well, it's not their choice. It's—"

"Don't feed me this bullshit, all right? I know when you're bluffing. Remember, I studied you."

That stung, and a surfeit of memories floated to Matt's consciousness, and a cold waved passed through his body. He clenched his muscles so it wouldn't show. Coyote always had that. Matt'd trained him, expecting the young man to show a kind of filial duty to him, but instead was stabbed in the back.

"See? You think I can't read that?" Coyote said, and flashed a grin. "You were never good at field work. Only a loyal dog."

"And what are you? A loyal pit bull?"

"Perhaps. But I'm being paid to do what I love. Whereas you…" Coyote jerked his finger at Matt. "Are swilling in the sewers, doing what your DNA tells you is wrong." He drank, finishing half a cup in a go. "I told you I studied you. How many people can say that they're doing what they love?" And he raised his hand, shaking it, grinning.

Matt sat down on the bed. He felt small, though he was still trying to convey some strength.

"You going to answer my question? You know I have explicit orders to end anyone who gets in my way?" Coyote said.

"Is that a threat?"

"No. I'm telling you that whatever you have planned, because I'm sure your weak heart didn't like what it saw in Greece, I will not be stopped," Coyote said and drank the rest of his drink, staring at Matt. "And if I am to be stopped, it's never going to be by someone like you. You just don't have the balls, old man."

Matt held the stare, but his chest crumpled.

"I will say that I'm surprised that you came out here," Coyote said and stood up. "But I know that's where your power stops."

"You'll let me know everything you do. I'm here to track this woman down. And if I remember one thing, it's that you're worthless at collection," Matt said. And he was filled with joy when he saw that this affected Coyote.

Coyote grinned and turned to the door. He stopped before opening and shook his now-empty cup. "Thanks. And I suppose I'll be seeing less of you?"

Matt wondered what he could say that would help him get a leg up on the assassin. "There's a mole."

Coyote didn't flinch. But Matt was certain he could see his pupils move.

"Did you hear me?" Matt said.

"I did. You're lying. Again."

"There is one. And they're telling Interpol everything."

This time Matt saw him flinch.

"Interpol knows?"

"That's right."

"Why didn't you tell anyone at the office?"

"And get all funding cut? You know how nervous they can be. No. I want to get this woman. So that's why I'm here." Matt paused and scratched his thigh, hoping that Coyote was buying all this.

"Why're you telling me?"

"We're in this together," said Matt.

"You're dreaming. I'll never work with you again."

That sounded ominous, and Matt felt that the Coyote didn't believe him, and that furthermore the man might not have liked that bluff. "Your room number," Matt said. He could feel his heart beating faster. He kept his eyes on Coyotes', though he wanted to see what the assassin's hands were doing.

"Oh? And who's good at collection now?" Coyote said and dropped the cup on the floor.

Matt shook his head, his fear and uncertainty morphing into a mock anger. "You're weak Coyote. And remember that I never taught you everything. But congratulations on finishing off an old man. Few people in the world can do that."

Coyote walked out.

When Matt heard the door click shut he leaned back and let out some air. He should've brought some poison. He stared at the blank ceiling. A tremor went through his body. Why was he here, and what did he hope to accomplish? Surely he wasn't trying to be a hero after spending most of his life trying to be the ultimate gray man. Another tremor when through him, and he knew now that he'd awoken a poisonous snake and that he should watch his back from this day forward because he was going to be hunted. Damn, why did he have to shake up the snake? And for what? For what.

Coral knocked on Drake's door. She was inside and a pair of kids, brown with odd colored clothes, ran by her.

Drake opened the door and stood blinking.

"Hi," she said. "I know it's late."

He stepped aside. Sophie meowed by his ankles and moved to rub her. She walked in, though she had never felt more unwanted.

"If you don't want me here..." she said.

His mind seemed to be elsewhere, and he jerked when she spoke. "No. It's fine," he murmured. "There's a little left over food."

She could smell an anger in the air he walked through. What about? She knew it was foolish coming here, but she didn't want to be alone.

Drake pulled out some plastic dishes with food. When he opened it up, the smell of curry hit her, and she tried not to wince. Not that she didn't like Indian food, but her stomach was upset from all the cogitation, and she didn't want spices making it worse.

"Something wrong?" Drake asked. There was definite hostility in his voice.

She tilted her head, her eyes touching all hints on his face. He was trying hard not to look into her eyes.

"What is it?" she asked. She couldn't for the life of her figure it out. And she couldn't figure out why she was here. Normally the slightest whiff of a man's recalcitrance and she was gone.

"Nothing," he said, looking at the food. He let out a sigh.

"Am I disturbing something?" she asked. For a second she pictured a woman coming out of a closet. Her heart dropped. Then she brushed that off, because it didn't make sense for him to hide anything from her since they barely knew each other, and she also wondered why she was so affected by his possible rejection. And knowing that she couldn't have that, she stepped away from him. "Well, how about I leave?"

"Stop," he said and grabbed her elbow.

Coral didn't usually allow a man to touch her like that, and not receive some sort of rebuke. But there was something about his voice's frequency that calmed her.

"Why?"

"I… I just don't want to be a doormat."

That surprised her. She realized that he was looking her in the eye. Her heart started to pound faster. And she couldn't think of anything to say.

"I'm tired of London and all the women looking for a quick one. I'm not that. So if that's what you're here for, go."

I'm not, she tried to say, but the words were stuck in her mouth. And she wanted to be closer. But she couldn't.

"Well…" he said, looking at her in a confused manner. "This is where you say something."

She still didn't say anything. The cat rubbed her calf, and she could feel it licking her. Inside, her heart fluttered and at the same time she felt calm. Almost like she was floating.

Now a half grin spread across his face. He was either nervous or cocky. Again she couldn't tell, and this made the room retreat and darken, and it pulled him into focus.

"You know," he said after a few seconds. "The reason, that I've heard humans invented language, was to get closer to each other, or at the least to let their intentions be known. What are your thoughts on that? I'm guessing you have a different theory?" His lips curled into a quarter smile.

She huffed out a half-laugh. "I don't."

"Oh, she speaks," he said.

His schoolboy grin forced her to take a step forward. She wanted his warmth on her.

"I'm not like those girls," she said, though she wasn't sure.

"Oh?" he said.

"I-I," she said and took another step towards him. She

wasn't certain what she should say. But she knew that right now she didn't feel like explaining herself, and so she wouldn't.

"I've been through a lot in the time you've seen me. Please..." she said and suddenly she could smell the charred ruins of her house, and she tried her hardest to hold back the tears.

Drake's face softened and he reached his arms around her and brought her in close. She squeezed back.

"Thank you," she said.

He led her to the sofa, the cat choosing to sit on Coral's lap.

"When you're ready, tell me what happened," he said.

She smiled. He ordered some fish and chips for takeout and they ate, the TV flashing images on mute.

"How's your book coming along?" she asked.

"I'm stuck," he said. "The character doesn't want to grow."

"What does that mean?" she asked. She could see a pain in his face that seemed too much for a story. Her life had been spent knowing this world, and she couldn't fathom why he was hurt over something that was make believe.

"All stories need a good character to drive them. That's the engine. Without that, you have a plot and nothing else."

She tried to process this.

"Do you read much?" he asked.

"Non-fiction. To tell you the truth I always saw fiction as a luxury."

"Thanks," he said and stuffed some remaining fries into his mouth.

"No," she said and touched his wrist. For a brief moment electricity ran through her body. She tried her hardest not to smile.

"I guess I never had much time. I always just researched for work."

He seemed to nod, but something told her that she'd hurt him.

"But I want to dive into it."

"What?" he asked.

"Books. Tell me what I should read."

"Oh," he said and placed a hand on his chin. He seemed lost for a second. "That's a hard one. I guess the classics are a good start."

"Don't tell me books that will have me running away."

"All right," he said. "That's fair. But how can I tell you a book I think is good, when I don't know you... I don't know what makes you tick?"

A warm feeling washed over her. "Then ask away." It was something she'd never said before. She'd always liked being a closed book. But with Drake and his cool placid eyes, and slow assured movements, and wide shoulders, she was willing to open up. Somewhere deep in her brain there was the old her telling her she was foolish and that the death of her father was making her be this way, but she wasn't going to listen to it.

"Where were you born?" he asked.

"Crete," she said. "You?"

"Oh, you're going to recommend some books for me too?" he asked.

"That's right. Non-fiction."

He laughed. She felt him move closer. The cat jumped to the floor, and she wondered if it was trained to do that.

"Here in London."

"Oh?" she said. "A fancy boy?"

"Hardly. I was an orphan."

"Just like Oliver Twist?" she asked. "Then I recommend tensile strengths of metal alloys. A great book."

He grinned. "I'll check it out. And Oliver Twist? Almost. Though these times are easier on the poor. I was raised by two NGO types in a small flat in South London. They'd me when I was twelve."

"Are they alive?" she asked.

"No. They were in Palestine for the second Intifada, and they were duly killed."

"What was that like?"

"I cried," he said. "They were the only people I knew who cared for me. But that was what they were made for."

"What's that?"

"Sacrificed at the altar of greater good."

That hit her hard. She didn't know if there was derision in his voice. "You don't agree with that?"

"I do. Otherwise I'd be working at a bank right now. No, I think it's necessary. I guess I'd rather still have them here. That dissonance makes me wonder." He stopped. The air between them crackled with electricity. And she could feel it prickling her skin.

"A beer. Or wine?" he asked as he stood up.

Annoyed that he would move away from her, she nodded her head. He walked off to the kitchen and came back with a box of wine.

He poured two glasses. They toasted, but she only took a sip. She didn't want the crispness of this feeling to dissolve into numbness.

"And your family?" he asked.

"I was born in Crete. Though I never knew my mother. My father took care of me."

"Oh?" Drake said and raised his glass. "We're a couple of orphans then?"

"Well. I consider him my real father," she said, then immediately regretted it when she saw Drake shrink.

"I didn't mean it like that," she said.

He nodded and took a huge gulp.

That distance grew between them made her cold. But she still liked this feeling of pouring out her soul. It felt so natural. "He died," she said.

"Just now," she said. "That's why I left so quickly."

"I'm so sorry," he said.

"Don't be."

"How old was he?"

"Sixty."

"What happened?"

She stared down at her glass of wine. Now it seemed like something she wanted to finish.

The cat jumped back on her lap and placed its paws on her chest. She smiled. She remembered that she was very likely being chased. Hunted. And that as much as she liked this man, any time spent with him was putting his life as risk.

"I'm sorry," she said. She shifted her weight, making to move from him. And again he placed his hand on her elbow.

"What is it?" he asked.

All the warmth had evaporated from her chest, and she felt an enormous guilt pushing her down into the ground.

"What is it?" he asked again.

"Promise to tell me if this freaks you out," she said.

He cocked his head and didn't say anything.

"My father was killed."

"How?" he asked.

That it didn't surprise him made her feel more confident.

"Whoever it was shot him, execution style. Then burned down the house. You don't look surprised," she said.

"I've been to many places in the world. My parents taught me that such things are commonplace. Unfortunately. What did your father do?"

She trembled as the truth bubbled up.

"You know people who were willing to sacrifice for a greater good?"

"Yeah?"

"That's what he did... me too."

Drake tilted his head, as if he expected more.

"His dream was to slowly, one by one, right the wrongs of

history. He was a great artist. And so he… we stole artifacts that had been stolen, and returned them to their rightful owners."

Drake leaned back and away from her. His eyes licked up her every move.

"I think that's what got him killed. But we've worked very smart. I can't see how, or who would have done that."

The cat jumped off her again and onto the table.

Coral waited for a response.

"Say something," she said.

"You're next?"

"That's right," she said.

"Will I be next too?"

Her guilt exploded… "I don't know," she said.

He let out air and looked at his cat. "I'm sorry about your father."

She almost heard him say but.

"But?" she said after a few seconds passed.

"No buts. I know the feeling. I'm guessing you can't go to the police with this?"

She shook her head. "I'm not certain they're not in on it. There were some strange men with the Greek Police."

"Of course," he said. His voice was tainted with anger.

She wondered from what. "If you want me to leave, I will."

"You're going to have to hit them back," he said. "Otherwise you'll never have peace."

"How's that?"

"My parents didn't die of a random attack, though that's how it was painted in the press. They called me a week before. They said the Israeli Shinbet was after them, and they were trying to leave."

"Why?"

"They were highlighting too many of their war crimes, why else?"

"And?"

"They were killed in a missile strike. Three houses they'd stayed in before that were blown up too. I tried to tell the police and the press here, but..." He swallowed, his adam's apple moving slightly, and poured himself another glass. "It was the first time I experienced a cover up. And though I'd never had much faith in the police, I lost it in all civilian institutions after that."

What was he trying to say?

"So we're going to have to hit these bastards, and hit them hard," he said.

They fell asleep, her in his arms.

Matt awoke, glistening with sweat. Sun was beating down on him. When he pulled back the curtains he saw a piece of sky with gray walls of clouds and a slit for the sun. The ray disappeared.

His stomach growled and he ordered room service. His intestines growled next so, with his day's newspaper, he walked into the bathroom and sat down on the toilet.

He remembered a time, during his first years as a spec ops soldier and having been in the infantry for so long, when he was surprised at being allowed to stay at so fancy a place. He'd also seen such luxury as inane. These days, though he welcomed the soft sheets to rest his weary joints, he still saw it as excessive. Plenty of people in his old neighborhood would never sleep in anything better than a trailer. He unfolded the Times newspaper and read the headlines. Economic news: Britain arguing about the proper place for cuts and when not to cut them.

The previous night's emotions flushed through his system. He had to find the girl. And he had to find Kim. They were supposed to meet up. But now he realized that he hadn't specified a link up. And he still had to contend with Coyote.

An object slid over the blanket in the other room and Matt froze. His heart thumping in his throat, he realized how nervous he was. He wiped up and walked into his room. Nothing. He stared at a piece of paper on the floor. It must have slipped. He relaxed and started stretching out to loosen his joints.

Breakfast came. Matt eyed the Somali boy who delivered his food. He didn't seem quite right, but he didn't seem sinister. His left eye twitched to the point that Matt felt sorry for him.

"Here," Matt said and handed him a substantial tip. "You seen anything suspicious?"

The boy's face startled and he started to stutter. Matt felt hopelessly sad for him and gave him an additional twenty pounds. The boy seemed to lighten up and left, bowing profusely.

Matt ate his scrambled eggs and bacon. The fat in the bacon was tender, and he chewed on it thinking about his next move. He was putting his career at risk, doing this. Not to mention how much the Coyote would eat him alive if he found out the real reason for his being here.

His fingers didn't notice it, but his eyes did. There was an obvious wrinkle in the paper. One that didn't make sense. He pushed it out, but it refused to disappear. His mind twinkled with the memory of fieldwork past. At the bottom of the page was a bump. He tore the page. It was the same page glued upon itself. He stared at the folded piece of paper.

He unfolded it. Picadilly Station. North Entrance. Ten.

It was typed. He tore the important parts to bits and threw it down the toilet. Who sent it? For all he knew Coyote could be testing him.

Matt looked outside. It was raining again. People on the street below rushed about, huddled in their long coats and under umbrellas.

He walked down the stairs, stopping every few seconds to see if there was someone following him. All the hairs on his skin stood on end.

Across the street, Matt bought himself a raincoat and umbrella and snuck out the back entrance. He wondered if Coyote had a team with him. Walking down the street, the wet rain penetrating the soul of his bones, he felt his phone vibrate. He picked it up.

"Matt?"

"Tim. How's it going?"

"They're not happy with you, bud," Tim said.

"Well, I have a job to do. If they don't like that—"

"I'm on your side," Tim said.

"Well I've seen Coyote, and he seems to be uncooperative."

"Of course. Why the hell would he get a nickname like that?"

Matt paused, looking at the reflection on a store window. There was a man, over six foot and stooped in a gray coat who was fifty paces behind him. Matt caught him staring, but made sure to not turn.

"Is Coyote alone?" Matt asked.

"Of course he is. Wh—"

"Why else would he get that name? I know," said Matt. Angry that Tim was being so difficult. "Did you get any more information on the man?"

"No. We have a couple guys tagging along with the local police, but even they're stuck. Man was a veritable ghost."

"Well, we have to catch this ghost," Matt said. He tried to sound gung-ho.

Tim's pause told him that his feign wasn't bought.

"And what about the girl?" Matt asked. He stopped at an intersection. He raised his hand for a taxi. One stopped and he jumped in. He held his phone so he could see the reflection. The man who was following him, with yellow eyes, picked up his pace.

"Picadilly," Matt said.

The taxi moved away. The man with the yellow eyes was trying to hail a taxi of his own when they turned the corner.

"Faster," Matt said. "And take as many turns as you can.

The large Indian man up front nodded his head like this was the most normal of requests and stepped on the accelerator.

"You there?" Tim asked.

"Sorry about that. What did the bosses tell you?"

"Christ, Matt. You know I can't say."

"Then why the hell did you call?"

"Well, they're going to call you in a second." Tim hung up.

"Drive around. Use a freeway, and then take me to

Picadilly," said Matt.

The man nodded again as if this too was perfectly normal.

Matt's phone rang. It was the boss.

"Hello?"

"What the hell do you think you're doing? You're heading off to interject your desk-sitting ass in a mission our owners want done their way?"

"I'm saving them from themselves," Matt said. He frantically thought of a good excuse. "This girl is a ghost and unless we want an international situation on our hands, I need to keep Coyote on a leash."

His boss scoffed. "How the hell do you plan on doing that?"

"I plan to find the girl and do a clean end," Matt said. "You want a burned house in London with an executed woman's body underneath it all?"

A long sigh sounded on the other end of the line. "Fine, fine. But you're on your own as far as the Coyote is concerned. The Texan likes him and isn't going to want his prized bulldog being leashed."

"You can't get him to at least —"

"I said you're on your own. Don't fuck this up. They wanted your head on a platter when they heard you were out there."

"I—"

"So don't give them a fucking excuse. I told them you were there for security, to help keep an eye on things."

"Security?"

"You didn't know? The Texan has almost all his Babylonian art in a showing there for the next few weeks. Your cover is that you're there to help and make sure it's safe. He doubled security around the damn place. Thinks the girl's out to get him."

Matt felt a wave of relief, and he relaxed. It was good to know that his boss was willing to help.

"Thanks," he said.

"Don't thank me. You need to be at the British Museum at ten."

"I can't."

"The fuck you can't. Be there at ten or be on a plane back here. Or…"

"All right. I'll head over there," Matt said.

"Don't mess up."

Before Matt could thank his boss again, the man hung up.

On the freeway he watched as the cars on the opposite side whizzed by. Nothing was going to be easy.

When the taxi arrived on the north entrance at Picadilly station, Matt handed the taxi driver some money.

"You want me to wait?" the taxi driver said.

"Sure…" Matt said. He was trying to keep an eye out for someone, anyone, who looked familiar or even vaguely out of place. But at such a busy entrance everyone, from the random vendors to lost tourists, looked suspicious.

"The best way is to wait at that corner," the taxi driver said.

Matt followed his finger and saw the dark corner of the entrance, right next to an alley. He nodded his head and stepped out. A fine mist fell; the cool touch on his face was welcome.

A throng of tourists and businessmen rushed by him. He couldn't recognize anything, but he felt someone tug his elbow. Hard.

He looked over and saw a young woman in a hoodie walking by him. He tried to reach over, but she was gone. The manner in which she walked reminded him of Kim. But was he certain? He made for her direction, but when the crowd cleared, she was nowhere to be seen.

He walked to the corner the taxi driver had pointed out and edged himself past a black vendor selling cell phone cases.

101

Aaron Grunn

"Five pounds," the man said, eyeing him through glassed-out eyes.

"No thanks," Matt said.

The man turned back to the sidewalk and called out to a businessman walking by. Matt realized that he smelled like curry.

And his pocket started to vibrate. He pulled out his phone from inside his coat and realized that it wasn't ringing. But a vibration was still tickling his thigh.

Matt reached down to his black pants and pulled out an unfamiliar phone. He answered the call.

"Hi there."

It was Kim.

"So that was you," Matt said. He craned his neck trying to see if there was anyone who was watching him.

"Don't look around," she said. "You'll seem like an amateur."

"I am," he said. It was funny how little he wanted to hide from this woman.

"Oh, I was kidding," she said. "We have a lead," she said.

"With the girl?" he said, and then wondered if perhaps Tim hadn't been truthful with him.

"Yes." Kim sighed and Matt could hear traffic in the background. It was similar to where he was. He stepped away from the vendor who seemed a little too quiet.

"Where?"

"Why didn't you tell me your boss had a show here?"

"I just found out," he said.

She sighed again. "You know we have to be honest with each other if this is going to work."

Matt knew that he couldn't be honest with her. Not if he wanted to get things done as he wanted. "Of course," he said. "So then tell me where she is."

"We don't have a current bead on her, but she's here. We have photos of her entering London."

"Can you send them to me?"

"Sure. They're much the same as the ones you have from before."

"Of course," he said. "And what about from the Underground?"

"She took a taxi," Kim said.

"So you're here to tell me that you've only confirmed that she's here?"

"Well, she came from Crete. Which means she saw what happened..."

Static picked up on the line. It sounded like a growl.

"Christ," Matt said. "You think she's here for revenge?"

"Why else?" Kim said.

Matt's mind raced. So his boss was right. But it surprised him that a thief would try to hit back. Most slinked back into the night. "Well let me know if you get anything," Matt said. He wanted to see her face to face. He wanted to talk to her about something other than this work of theirs. But he knew that was foolish.

"I will. You too. Keep this phone. It can't be hacked."

"Fine. You keeping MI5 informed?"

"Of course. They're the ones helping us. They want a clean cut. And they hardly need the fanfare."

Matt felt a drop in his heart. So she *was* just like his bosses. "Clean cut?" he said.

"Yeah. Nothing like Crete. Please."

"Of course."

The line went dead. And Matt felt absolutely disgusted with himself. Why was it that she couldn't see this situation for what it was?

"You want a smoke man?" the vendor said.

Matt nodded his head and took the cigarette from the man.

"You look like you need it?" the vendor said and smiled.

As Matt inhaled, his mind relaxed, and he tried to think of

103

a way to find the woman. "Thanks," he said and pulled out a five pound note.

"No," the vendor said.

"Give me that case," Matt said.

The vendor handed it to him and Matt walked back to the taxicab.

The driver was talking on the phone when Matt stepped inside.

"She didn't show?" the taxi driver said.

"No," Matt said.

"Sorry."

"Not to worry." Matt slammed the door shut and shivered as the warm air of the taxi encased him.

"Where to next?"

"I'm not sure. Your shift over soon?"

"It is," said the taxi driver.

"You know a good cafe or pub?"

"I know just the place," said the man and he shifted the taxi into gear.

Matt leaned back and rubbed his temples. He had no clue as to how to find this woman. Not without the weight of his company behind him. "Oh wait," Matt said. "Take me to the British Museum first."

"You too, eh?" The taxi driver smiled.

Matt wondered what that meant. "What would you do if you were looking for someone?"

"Me?" the taxi driver asked.

"There's a start. I mean, you know this city well, don't you?"

"I suppose. But it's mainly the streets I know."

"You have no way of—"

"I did once look for a girl. And I found her."

"And how did you do that?"

"You have to find the groups she hangs out with. Then start asking questions. May I ask why you're looking for this person?"

"It's a woman," Matt said. "And… I'm going to save her life."

The taxi driver nodded slowly. "That's a fine thing to do."

"Shouldn't that be the least we do for another human?"

The taxi driver pulled over in an empty alley. What had he done? Being so foolish as to open up to a stranger?

The man turned. He had a turban on, and his face had melted its fat a long time ago.

"I'm sure it's at risk to your life, isn't it?"

Matt wondered what he would do if the man burnished a weapon. It'd been ages since he'd gone through a hand-to-hand class.

"Sure."

The man's eyes pierced Matt's.

"You're ex-mil, aren't you?"

"How—"

"I was too. India."

"Kashmir?"

"Among other places. Iraq?"

"Among other places," Matt said.

"I had to move out of that world," said the taxi driver.

"I should have."

"And now you have to save this girl."

"It certainly appears that way," said Matt. An odd feeling was replacing the earlier dread, and he felt more connected to the world, and felt more strongly about helping this girl.

"I'll try to help you out anyway I can," said the taxi driver.

"Thanks. But there's danger involved."

"My life?"

"Yes."

"I've done that before," said the taxi driver.

"A war is different from these sorts of deaths. In these you will be trampled upon even after they kill you. It's how they work."

The man seemed to consider it, then turned, shifted the taxi into gear and drove in silence until they arrived at the British Museum.

"Here's my card," said the taxi driver. "Should you need a discrete driver."

"Thank you," said Matt. He stepped out, a ray of sun warmed him. He wanted to sip down with a glass of whiskey and forget all this. And he also wanted to go back home. One glance at the taxi driver, who was waving, and Matt felt strong again. He stuffed the card into his coat pocket and walked into the museum. This was something that old soldiers simply understood.

As Coral wrote out the list of all the past places she'd stolen from, Drake leaned over her shoulder and whistled.

"Well, weren't you a naughty girl."

She slapped his hand that rested on her shoulder. "Quiet you,' she said.

He chuckled and walked into the kitchen. Sophie jumped on Coral's lap and pushed her nose into Coral's neck.

"Not now, little one," Coral said and pushed the cat away. She wrote down a few more places she'd stolen things from, and the names associated with those items. Something in her gut started to worm its way up to her heart, and increased her blood pressure. Her breaths shortened and her head tightened, and the hand holding the pen shook. She tried to hold her breath. What was so hard about writing a few names? She tried to reason her way through it. Was it that she'd kept this secret for so long? She'd disciplined herself to never talk about a hit after it was done. Never. That minimized the risk of being listened to by the wrong people. And now she was risking all that. She reminded herself that she was here to find the people who killed her father, and to do that, she would have to throw away all the rules they had from before. After all, they hadn't worked for him.

"Do you want a brew?"

"No. I'm fine," she said. Hearing his voice calmed her down. She still wasn't sure why, but she trusted him completely. It was as if they'd known each other their whole lives.

"I meant a tea," he said.

"Oh. Then yes," she said and went back to writing. When she was done, she showed Drake the list. He whistled again. "You really stole from the Iranians?" he said.

"That's right," she said. Small memories of what went down in Tehran hit her. She grinned. "It wasn't easy," she said.

"I'd imagine." His fingers traced over a names, then came

back to the top. "I would think we should stay with the most recent ones, but let's do a search on each name," he said and shifted to his laptop. One by one, he entered the names. He crossed all but ten out.

"Why'd you cross them out?

"These were people who only had a few million in their banks, or who didn't achieve their wealth through nefarious means," he said.

"How can you tell?"

"Well. Most billionaires aren't crossed out, unless we're talking about the extremely talented."

"Okay," she said, not sure, but deciding that he probably knew more than she did in this matter.

He narrowed one eye at her. "If someone's a billionaire in an established business, how do you think they got to the top?"

She knew.

"And now, let's see who has access or ties to state services, or mercenaries," he said.

"How do you find that?"

"I can hack into newspapers and businesses and look. They have that information kept from the public."

She didn't want to believe that was true. He hunched over the computer and started to peck at his keyboard.

Coral sat down on the sofa and, with Sophie back on her lap, stroked the cat. Being in Drake's presence was such a natural thing that she wondered how she ever managed without him.

"Here," he said. She walked over to him. With a hand, he rubbed his traps. She slapped his hand away and started to massage for him.

"All of them?" she said.

"Yup," he said. But these four had access to similar resources," he said. "And they're the most recent. Well, them and the Iranians," he said.

"So we're down to them," she said. She didn't know which one sounded worse to have chasing her.

"This name," Drake said and pointed at the latest hit. "There's something about it that rings a bell."

"I don't see why," Coral said.

"Hold up," Drake said and ran out to his bedroom. A second later he appeared with a catalogue. "Andy gave this to me. He's always trying to get me to come out and see the place after it's closed."

Drake flopped the catalogue in front of Coral.

Coral stared at the catalogue. She couldn't believe her luck. The Texan had a large amount of items at the British Museum on show. But she didn't know if that was more than a coincidence.

"Hold on," Drake said and went to grab his coat.

"What's wrong?" she said. She didn't want him to leave.

"Andy's not working today. I'm going to ask him about the security."

"Why? I don't get it."

"Don't you see?" he said. "The last hit you did was at his place, right?"

"Right," she said. "So?"

"So why would he be so bold as to show everything all at once, like this, unless he knew you were on the run?"

"He could just be cocky," she said.

"That's rarely the case," said Drake. "And if he's after you, I bet there's a bunch of extra men at the British Museum."

She watched as he walked out, and she could feel her head tightening. Was it *that* hard to watch a man she just met walk out? She knew now that the strings from her heart to him were strong. So what was she doing allowing him to walk down this dangerous route with her? What would she do if he died? Her heart stuttered. She sat down and stroked Sophie, waiting.

After what seemed to be more than a few minutes, the lock started to jiggle. Before Coral could get up and open the door, Drake stepped in. His face looked shaken. Andy walked in behind him.

Coral, sensing that something was wrong, looked around the apartment for anything that could be used as a makeshift weapon.

"Hi," she said. Andy's face seemed stern.

"I'm sorry," Drake said. "He insisted on coming here."

Andy's face lightened and he hugged Coral. "So you giving him problems?"

Coral forced a smile. She definitely didn't want another person pulled into this.

Andy raised his eyebrows, heavy lines flashed across his face. "Come on, I'm not a fool. Why else would you be at the British Museum at night, after it was closed. Then have more questions?"

Drake hung back in the kitchen. "Tea?" he asked.

"Of course," Andy said. He pointed at the sofa.

Coral sat down. What was she to do? She liked Andy. But was he going to turn her into the police?

"I'm not going to try and stop you. And my lips will be sealed on the entire matter," Andy said, sitting next to Coral. "You have my word. But, I'll warn you that they know you're coming."

"How's that?" Coral said. Her spirits dropped further. She wondered if there was a photo of her circulating in the Museum.

"We have a whole host of outside security for this show for the... the Texan. When I started to talk to their security they said they were on the look out. That they had been robbed by a female thief, and they expected her to hit again."

"And?" Coral asked.

"They knew you were in London. But that's it."

She felt sick now, like her guts were tying themselves into

knots.

The kettle screeched and Coral jumped. A few seconds later, Drake came with three cups of tea.

They all raised their glasses in a toast. Drake sat next to Coral and placed his arm on her shoulder. She was thankful for that. Her insides settled, and she felt stronger.

"Was there a photo?" Drake asked.

Coral, expecting Drake to freak out, was thankful that he was calm. His body heat warmed her up, providing more energy for her.

"No," said Andy. "There was something fishy about the whole thing. Like they were setting up a trap. We wanted to tell local police, but they refused. Said they had it under control. But that's my point. Even if they don't have a photo, there are now several parallel security systems on all his artifacts. There's no way you're going to get past it all."

"Is that it?" she said. She felt bad that it came out so rudely.

"That's about it," said Andy. He leaned back and sipped his tea. For a minute there was nothing but the sound of sips and cups clanking on saucers.

"They didn't mention anything else?" Drake asked, looking at Coral. "Nothing about revenge?"

Andy shook his head before cocking it.

Coral raised her eyebrows at Drake, she didn't want to get Andy any further into this mess. For a few seconds silence pervaded throughout the apartment. Coral's mind was still trying to put together what Andy's information meant.

"We can tell him," Drake said.

"I'm a grown man," said Andy.

"No," Coral said. "We're talking about murder."

Andy shrugged. "And? I'm an old man. I see death everywhere." And he tapped his hips. "One more fall and I'm out." He grinned.

Drake chuckled. "Well I think it was the Texan, why else

111

would he have all the extra security. And if he's setting up a trap—"

Coral glared at Drake, trying to get him to shut up.

"What?" said Drake. "It's obvious."

"Maybe he's just scared," Coral said. "But we shouldn't talk about this in front of—"

"Well it's too late now. I know. You've robbed from this guy before. And now he's looking to get you," Andy said.

"Maybe," Coral said.

Andy rolled his eyes. "I could use one more adventure."

"They killed my father," Coral said. "This is not a game."

Andy whistled. "Well I'm in. And I'm sure Taj would be as well."

"Andy," said Coral. "This is serious."

"Christ," Andy said. "I want to help. And besides, I've seen worse, and been in worse."

Coral wanted to hear Drake say something on her behalf, but she only heard him sip. She still didn't want to see two older men, who had nothing to do with this, get hurt.

"I don't know," she said.

"I do," said Andy. "With all the security systems... You'll need me to do a proper analysis. This isn't an ordinary Museum robbery now." His chest seemed to puff out.

"We don't even know if it's the person we want to go after," said Coral. "It might be a coincidence."

"I doubt it," said Andy. He shifted a leg and rubbed his knee. "From the way they were acting, they wanted to catch you. On their own. That means they want to snuff you."

"See?" said Drake. "I'm with Andy on that one. It has to be the Texan."

"Fine," said Coral. "But I really don't want you involved, Andy. What if something happens to you? Or if they go after your family?"

That seemed to give Andy pause. He stroked his head. "Well, that's a risk. But to be fair, my family isn't on the records," Andy said. Coral moved to speak, but Andy raised his hand. "But let me tell you this. I've worked a long time at this museum, and there are plenty of good rich people who acquired their art the proper way, and there are folks who could only have gotten it the wrong way. I read about you. Now I may be old, but I want to help you. And if you don't, I'm going to raise a big stink about it." He grinned.

Coral let out some air. She could feel some tears forming in her eyes. "Thank you Andy," she said.

"No, thank you," Andy said and slowly got up, his knees popping.

"We're going to recon the place," Coral said. "Now."

"Wear a disguise," said Andy. "I've a shift tonight. I'll find out the systems, and all. Taj'll look for any sort of roving outside patrols. That way we'll know if they're on the look out in the neighborhood."

"Bloody lot you're doin'," Drake said.

"Of course," said Andy and winked at Coral. "So you've really got him, eh?"

Coral blushed; she didn't know what to say.

Drake was silent.

"She's the kind that's worth the trouble," said Andy.

"Andy," Drake said, his voice was low.

Coral glanced at Drake; he was almost beet red. What he was thinking?

Andy left, and Drake flopped on the couch. "So the museum then?"

Coral stepped up to Drake. There were tingles all over her body. "Let's go," she said.

She walked to the bathroom and put on some fake contacts as well as makeup to change some aspects of her face. When she was done, she walked out.

"You look different," said Drake. "But do you think it'll be enough?"

She didn't reply, certain that they wouldn't have a photo

of her. Outside, the sky was full of grey wispy clouds. "What are we looking for?" asked Drake.

But Coral didn't answer. She had to get into a professional state of mind. This wasn't going to be easy. She relaxed, doing yoga breathing exercises, and she realized that she might be going into deeper more treacherous waters than ever before. Her entire body tightened, expecting a punch from life.

Matt walked into the museum and walked right up to a security guard. "Can I talk to your boss? I have a meeting with someone."

The security guard, dark and tall, looked over Matt, then turned and talked into his radio.

A few seconds later a short bald man in a black suit came running down the steps.

"Hi, sir," the man said in a confused accent.

Matt, recognizing a few faces, grew angry with himself for showing up.

"Here are your men and details," said the bald man.

Before Matt could say anything, the bald man bounced away, and all Matt could see was a shining head, reflecting the ceiling lights as he scurried away.

"How are you, sir?"

Matt turned to see a crew-cut man, with the usual military demeanor-stench hanging off him.

"Hi..."

"James, sir."

"James," Matt said and shook his hand. It was a too-firm handshake, and Matt wanted more than ever to leave.

"You in charge of the security here?" asked Matt. The smell of the man's fresh-shower cologne annoyed Matt. He wanted to hit the Underground and head to someplace dirty and dangerous, like the South end.

"No sir," James said, with a curious look on his face. "I'm in charge of us and our section."

"The Texan's," Matt said.

"That's right sir," said James, standing tall.

"Show me what you got," Matt said, knowing he had to give the appearance that he cared.

They walked through a few rooms, by some Greek Statues.

"Here sir," said James, and he started to drone on about the various security measures being used. Roving guards, pressure plates, wires, cameras, back up batteries, heat sensors.

Matt could see that they had at least twenty of their own security men, some in civilian clothes, in the room. The Texan must have been really scared to have this many men here. All of them, Matt noted, looked like James. Matt bumped into one of the museum's actual guards. He seemed old. As he stepped away, Matt realized that the man was listening to their conversation. The hairs on his back stood up, and he wanted to alert James, but he decided not to say anything.

James droned on. About some laser security system that was activated at night. None of it was anything that Matt hadn't heard before. "What's activated during the day?" Matt asked.

James stared at him for a few seconds. "There are some detectors for people who get too close, but we have two men on each major artifice."

"That's it?" Matt asked, trying to act surprised.

"And some weight sensors, and some cameras," James said. He seemed worried. "Do you think we need to add something?"

"No," Matt said, suppressing a smile. "Go on."

James thought for a second. "Because I've heard that she's good."

"She is," James said. "But she's not superhuman."

James continued his drone.

Matt spaced out. The items on display glittered under their glass cases. He wondered how much had been stolen, and how much had been acquired legally.

Twenty minutes later, as James introduced Matt to each one of his security men, Matt chewed his tongue, bored out of his mind.

His thoughts lost all intensity, and his eyes rolled over to a tall blond wearing shorts that were not too far from underwear. His eyes moved over half a meter, and his heart stopped. There was the woman, with a good disguise, and a man on her arm.

"And that brings our tour to a close. Anything else?" James said, moving into a stiff repose.

"Nope. Looks like you have this under control. Give me your number," Matt said. As soon as he had the information, he left. He waited outside for the woman. His hands sweated as he kept an eye on every person coming out.

An hour later, he fell on his hotel bed. He couldn't believe what had just happened, and his heart still pounded in his chest. He took big gulps of air, and slowly brought his fears under control. He'd never done something this out of line before. He closed his eyes. How did he ever get stuck in this job? How did he ever get stuck in this life?

After a few minutes, when he knew that sleep was not going to come to him, he stood up and watched a few people on the street. He wished he were like them. Ignorant of what was happening. Of the evil that boiled just underneath the ground. He *really* wished he were them. But it was too late to turn back. No one ever tells you that there's no turning back. Once you see this side of mankind it'll be too late. He placed his hand on the cold windowpane. Was he getting weak with time?

Fog from his mouth blurred his view. He *was* getting old. As if to answer him, his joints moaned. For some reason he remembered the smell of Kim in that car. But she was young. Just new to the whole circus that was the intel world, and she was full of energy. She'd never see things the way he did. And if she did she'd be no good at her job. She seemed like she wanted nothing more than to climb the career ladder that was placed in front of her. He chuckled. So that's what he was? A broken machine.

He considered ordering a bottle of whiskey, but he reminded himself that he needed to stay clear. For all he knew, the Coyote could be somewhere near. Again his mind drifted to Kim, the curve of her thighs. He tried to brush it away. It was best to be alone right now.

Someone knocked on the door. It was soft. Matt immediately thought of the Coyote. He wondered if he was willing to face him today. His hand started to tremble. No, he wasn't ready. He walked to the fridge and pulled out a drink. Another knock. He should've bought a weapon by now, what was he thinking?

"Coming," he said.

He opened the door, half expecting that gun of Coyote's to be staring him down. Instead there was a woman, in a tight raincoat. She was smiling. It took him a second to realize that it was Kim.

"Come in," he said, though he wasn't sure if he was speaking. She walked in. Her smile turned into the stern face he was used to.

"Good to see you," he said.

"You too. How's London treating you?" she said and walked up to the window and drew the curtains.

"It's fine. You get any new information?" he asked.

"No," she said, shaking her head. "This one's a ghost. I'm surprised the father was ever found. Have you found anything?" she asked.

"No," he said, knowing that he was lying. Seeing her was making him weaker and stronger than ever at the same time. This dichotomous feeling made him dizzy, and he sat down on his bed.

"You all right?" she asked.

"I'm fine," he said.

She looked at the small bottle of whiskey he'd pulled out. "You sure?"

He wasn't certain why, but there was genuine concern in her voice. She was probably worried about his mission-ready status. "I'm fine," he said. He could smell her perfume. It was

118

barely noticeable underneath the smell of her sweat, though both were sweet. He felt blood rushing to his groins, and he tried to fight it. He wasn't being professional.

She looked at him. He tried to maintain eye contact, but the room seemed to spin around her, and in the periphery he could see her lips pulsating. She removed her coat, and through her business suit he could see the outlines of her thighs, and he still tried to stare into her eyes, because she was staring into his, but blood was rushing past his ears, and he was very certain that she could notice this.

"So what's the next step?" he said.

"We will help you keep an eye on the Texan's artifacts in the Museum," she said. "All that security is great, but it isn't going to stop this woman."

"She's good, but she's not a witch," he said. Part of him wondered why it was that Kim was here, if this was all she had to say.

She smiled. He looked over at the bottle. What was wrong with him? He was no stranger to women, but this one was tearing him apart.

"That's it?" she said.

Matt could see the outline of the top of her breasts over her dress. Her skin seemed so smooth, and he tried to breath deep, and tried to think of something that would make his intentions seem professional.

She stepped forward. Her head was tilted. She smirked.

His heart in his mouth, Matt tried to swallow, then realized that it was too loud, that he had gulped. Then he stood up, so close that her breasts just barely touched his torso. She didn't flinch, and her stare was hard. He could hear his own heart beating hard. He could feel his cock move, fill. He raised a finger and touched her chin. He realized that she was breathing as hard as him, and he could see the rise and fall of her chest, but he kept his eyes on hers. This was pulling his muscles off the bone, and it hurt, but he liked it.

119

He let his finger trail on her jawline, then up to her jet-black hair. The silky strands fell forward from her ear. She blinked. He needed that moment of tenderness. Her lips were bright red now, as were her cheeks. He trailed down one strand of hair, and he leaned in. He moved past her lips, hearing her gasp, and he smelled her hair. It was damp from rain, but smelled clean. He sniffed her neck. That sweet-sweat smell was strong, and he moved back and saw her face burning. Her pupils wide.

Blood gushed all over his body, and he tried to control himself, but it was a losing battle. He looked into her eyes. He could smell something else on her, something sweet. He leaned in and touched her lips. She gasped. He kissed her.

He expected to be in control, but she grabbed his face, and playfully tapped his cheek. There was a grin on her face, and he felt confused. Her nails dug into the side of his neck; they moved down, under his shirt, to his back. He could feel her grinding on his cock, and the spark in her eyes made her seem like a completely different person. With one swift movement, she lifted her hands. He could hear the buttons on his shirt pop, and the tearing of the silk-and-something cloth. She paused, staring at his bare torso. The cool of the room pushed a tremor over his skin. He watched her eyes dart all over, almost like she was studying him. He knew he should try and say something smooth, but he took in her heat, and smell, feeling like it was so much a dream.

She smiled, and slapped him on his cheek. He felt angry for the slightest of moments, but she tapped her hip into his, and he couldn't think of anything else but her, or *it*, and he pulled her closer, letting out a sound that was close to growling, though he wasn't certain. He undid her buttons and took off her shirt. Her bra, black, wrapped on top of a tight waist. He could see the swoop of her hips, and he leaned into her ear.

"That's beautiful," he said.

She narrowed her eyes at him. For a second he thought she was angry.

"Thank you," she said, playfully biting her lip.

He kissed her all over her body, then undid her top pants. She slapped his hand when he was done with the button. She pushed him down, and he felt his pants come off, and he felt his boxers slip off. Her nails dug into the side of his belly and the warmth of her breath was between his legs, her mouth on him. She shook and he trembled.

When she was done, she stood up on the bed above him, and did a strip tease. He watched, and when he wanted to say something, she placed a finger on her lips.

She squatted down, and he felt her hot inside. Though part of him wanted to say something about a condom, he decided not to. Felt everything of her. A small tremor run over his body. He watched enthralled with this woman possessed as her hair bounced, and her hips ground into him. He placed his hands on her ass, amazed still at her petite waist and thick hips. But her eyes were closed the entire time, and he had the feeling that he was not the one she wanted to be with. He held off until she spasmed, arching her back and feet, before he came inside her.

She pushed herself off him and walked to the bathroom. He lay there for a few seconds then grabbed a tissue off the nightstand, wiping his cock and standing up, feeling a huge need to sleep. He stared at the flakes of dried juice on his member and an odd joy welled up. He reminded himself that such a relationship wasn't meant to last.

The toilet flushed and she came out with a pack of cigarettes and a bathrobe on. "Mind if I smoke?" she asked. The cold voice from before was back. For some reason it felt like stab to his heart.

Matt shrugged and watched as she walked to the window and opened it. The cold wind hit him hard and he looked for and grabbed another bathrobe from the closet. She handed him a cigarette, already lit, and he inhaled it.

"Unfiltered?" he said and examined the brandless pack she had.

"Why not?" she said, still looking outside. She seemed unaffected by the cold.

"What brand?" he asked, sucking in the oak-flavored tobacco.

"Oh, you Americans and your brands," she said, almost angry now. She rolled her eyes.

He felt hurt, and must of looked it because she looked him over and forced a smile.

"I was only kidding," she said. "Even us South Koreans are like this now. It's the way of the world." She didn't seem to like this.

He nodded, trying to think about what kind of person she was and whether he should tell her anything about the woman at the museum. "Why were your eyes closed?" he asked, surprising even himself, as he hadn't expected to sound so spurned.

She looked at him, again examining him. "I don't want a relationship," she said.

He felt his heart drop, but bit his inside cheek to make sure it didn't show. "Of course. And we have a professional mission here," he said.

"That's right," she said and took a few puffs from her cigarette.

A car honked in the distance, and he wondered what it was about her that still made his heart rate increase.

"You ever loved anyone, Matt?"

Matt thought for a second. He had lusted, and he had cared, but he wasn't sure about love. "I—"

"I'll take that as a no." She chuckled. "One knows or they don't.

Again he felt hurt, but he tried to ignore it. "You?" he said.

"I did once. Before I joined Interpol." She indicated at the window with her head, though Matt wasn't sure what she meant.

"Once," he said, trying to gauge her body language. When she wanted to be cold, she could be cold. There was nothing he could do to change that.

"I met him when BASE jumping," she said. She looked up at him, and he nodded.

"I never," he said. She seemed like she wanted to be prodded.

"I did. Back when I worked for Korea's Service."

Matt didn't know much about that unit, so he kept quiet.

"It was a way to relax and to clear your head. It's a kind of meditation."

Matt knew about meditation, and perhaps running was his, but having jumped out of planes earlier in his life, he couldn't see how jumping off buildings with only one chute was meditation. This meant, in his eyes, that she was a speed freak, and that was always a warning sign for greater issues. He moved closer to her.

"He was the same. He loved it and during my time off we traveled and snuck into different structures to jump out of more and more dangerous places. Then one day, on a jump we hadn't planned," she said and stopped to take a hit of a cigarette. "We jumped out of a hotel building. A window like this." She pointed at the window again. "It seemed so easy. Especially when compared to what we'd done before."

Matt placed his hand on her shoulder. He wasn't sure how she was going to react.

"It's funny how life can switch from pure happiness to sadness... or nothing... like that," she said.

Matt took a seat next to her.

"I couldn't mourn him, or go to the funeral. He worked for the Chinese government."

"I'm sorry," he said.

"It's not for you to be sorry about," she said curtly.

Matt took his hand off her shoulder.

"I'm sorry," she said. "I didn't mean it."

"That's fine."

"But I couldn't work for my people after that. Not directly at least. So I came to Interpol."

He wondered what was going to happen between them, then decided that he needed to stop thinking that way. He flicked his cigarette into the cold outside, and she did the same. Several taxis streamed by. He stood up and held his hand out.

She took it and he led her back to the bed. Under the blanket, her warmth next to him, he felt better. Again she took control of him. Used him. He liked it. Wanted more. But she acted like there was someone else in the room, and she kept her eyes closed the entire time. He surprised himself when he didn't feel slighted this time. When they were done, Matt pushed the blankets away from him. They were wet and clammy. Entirely at ease with the world, he reminded himself that he shouldn't fall for her.

She lit another cigarette, blowing smoke into the air. He watched the trail, and lit himself a cigarette as well. The silence between them was laced with the thought of her past lover. Why had she closed her eyes? But as he watched her contemplating an unknown, he knew that she was just the kind of woman he would love to fall for. And when she turned her back to him, he traced the curve of her impossible body and blood once more rushed to his cock.

She didn't talk again and guided him inside. When he was done, he noticed that his cigarette was burning the pillow. He ran to the bathroom and returned with a cup of water. She watched the smoke rise up from the fabric. When he dosed it she still watched it, impassively. He threw the pillow on the ground. Her coldness was like an iron fist gripping his heart.

She grinned; it looked forced. He relaxed and felt joy

lifting him off his feet.

"You look happy," she said.

"I am," he said. He didn't want to ask her about her happiness because it might be a slap to his manhood. "You doing all right?"

"I'm all right," she said.

He moved himself next to her. The sheet of her naked body still aroused him, and he was surprised that he wasn't exhausted yet. Only a few strands of flesh in his body protested. She tapped it.

"Still?" she said, and smiled. He was sure it was genuine.

He thought of a million things to say and settled on grinning. She stared at his eyes, darting back and forth.

"We should play go again sometime," she said.

"We should. Though it will mainly you be teaching me."

She observed him. "You have a lot to learn," she said.

He wasn't sure if she was talking about go.

"How do you like your job?" she asked.

"It pays," he said.

"That is the definition of a job."

"I'm good at it," he said. His mind now shifted to whether he should tell her his plan. "And you? You like Interpol?"

"They do a lot of good," she said.

At least she considered them separate. "I guess neither of us is going to answer the question properly, right?" he said.

She raised her eyebrows. "So we must be good at what we do then."

"You still believe in the overall mission of your organization. Don't you?" he said.

"I do..." Her mind seemed to dart off. "You don't?"

He wondered if it was wise to tell her this. "Perhaps."

"Yes or no."

"No."

She sighed. "You know your problem in go? What

separates you from the best?"

"I haven't played enough?"

She sighed again. "No."

She didn't say anything, and the sounds of the street floated in and cracked Matt's cocoon. He decided to hold out until she spoke.

"You problem," she said. "Is that you can't see the overall picture. That is a very important part. To see globally, strategy, and get there locally, tactics. You are the kind of person who gets lost in the feeling of tactics. That makes you predictable. You never see the strategy."

That hurt, and he could feel his heart moan. He wasn't even certain if she was talking about go, his job, or his life. He had, of course, suspected something like that for all three. And he knew that he would only ever be the middle manager who saw small details, small feelings, and never the bigger picture. Was that what she was saying. And his heart lurched as he wondered if she could be talking about his plan here in London.

"I didn't mean to hurt you," she said and caressed his jaw.

"That's fine," he said, his voice low. But she had already cut him deeper than she could ever imagine. Anger bubbled up.

"So what about information?" she said and lit a cigarette, handing him the lit one, and lighting her own.

"Coyote is here. In this hotel," he said. And it surprised him, that no matter how much she had just hurt him, he still wanted to open up to her.

"Oh?" she said and tilted her head.

"Yes. And the Texan has a show here."

"I know that," she said, waving her hand.

"I'm in charge of the security there. It's a good cover, though not planned."

She nodded. "And what of this woman?"

"The one you want arrested, or taken away without

fanfare?" he said, hoping to hurt her.

"Yes," she said, not missing a beat.

"No clue. She's good. But I doubt that she will come after the museum. That would be suicide."

"If she's as good as you say, then it won't be long before she figures out who paid the Coyote to do what he did. And then what?"

Matt knew what he wanted to happen, but he reminded himself not to be that big of a fool. "If we have to use Coyote as bait, then so be it."

"Is that wise?" she said.

"What do you know?"

"Seems that we know about the same," she said. He must have looked annoyed because she continued: "Trust me. I'll tell you as soon as we find out anything."

"And what are your bosses' orders?"

"Same as before," she said. "You really are a romantic, aren't you?"

"What do you mean?" he said, trying to toughen up his appearance.

"You know... Remember what I said about you weakness. Romanticism is fine. But you shouldn't forget that you don't have the ability to see everything."

Again he wondered if she knew. But he didn't ask. And in a second she was up and putting on her clothes. He watched, sad that she wasn't going to stay, that he wasn't going to feel her warmth for a night. He bit his tongue when he wanted to ask her if she was going to come back.

She looked over her shoulder. "Thank you. When you get more information, call."

She was back to being cold.

"You too," he said, his voice rusty.

She walked over to the whiskey bottle on the table and threw it at him. "Have fun."

It seemed more mean spirited than he expected from her,

but she was gone before he could throw some anger her way. When the door clicked shut, he opened it and took a drag. He looked down and saw the flakes of her juices still left over. Deep down he could sense that he already missed her, was attached. He headed for a shower, making sure the chain was on the door.

Back at Drake's apartment, Coral had a shower. The reconnaissance hadn't gone as well as she expected. The security was too tight. At least twenty plain-clothes security men were wandering around that room. It had made her skin crawl, but also it made her realize that it was most likely the Texan who ordered the hit on her father. Anyone who was that careful about his toys, had to be guilty of something. And that knowledge made her angry and tore down her fear. She wanted to get back at him, and she knew that taking away his precious artifacts, denying him the immortality that all rich men wanted—usually in the form of a heartless library-museum—would hurt him more than anything. But that also meant that she needed to find out as much about him as possible. When she stepped out of the shower, got dressed, Drake was preparing dinner.

"I hope you like bass," he said without so much as looking up at her.

"That's fine," she said. "I'm going to make a phone call. Where's the nearest pay phone?"

"Down the street," he said, pointing with his hand.

She paused for a second. She really couldn't tell what Drake's intentions were. Here he was helping her on an extremely dangerous assignment, and he didn't seem to ask for so much as a thank you. He was kind, but now she was wondering if he was too kind. Why wasn't he looking at her? She decided to think about that later and stepped out, grabbing a coat before.

She made her way to a pay phone. Deciding that it was too close, she hailed a taxi. It was a brisk night, but at least it wasn't raining. After several minutes, she pointed out a pay phone and was dropped off.

"Hello?" the voice on the other end replied. It sounded haggard and tired.

"It's me," she said. She knew better than to say her name. She hoped that Alexandros had found out something. "I need information."

Alexandros exhaled heavily onto the mouthpiece. She was sure he sounded sick, perhaps worse, but perhaps her nerves were too frayed to tell the difference.

"What do you mean?" he asked.

That didn't sound right. Was he trying to tell her something? Was he too being watched?

"Can you talk?" she asked.

Now she was certain she heard rustling, except it sounded like there was more than just one person with him. Perhaps it was a romp? She couldn't be certain. And she couldn't be certain how to find anything out. But the danger words. Why hadn't he used them? Her heart started to beat fast and the air weighed down on her shoulders. She leaned against the pay phone booth's wall.

"I can," he said.

"The names I gave you. Did you find anything out?"

Now she was certain she heard rustling in the background. But it wasn't the rustling of someone who was trying to be quiet. She was sure Alexandros was under duress.

"The last name I gave you. Can you find out more?" she asked.

"Don't call here," he said. Then let out a groan.

He was in trouble.

"Are you okay?" she asked, feeling foolish for asking that.

"They know you're in London. It was him—"

A gunshot. Some gruff voices. The rational part of her brain was telling her to hang up, or else they would trace the call. But she had to hear if Alexandros was all right. When everything remained silent, she was sure he was dead. And she was sure they were about to trace her. She hung up, and ran away from the booth. After a few minutes, she hailed another taxi. Several taxis later, she was back with Drake.

"Food's ready," he said and let her in. "You're soaked." He cocked his head. "But it's not raining..." He ushered her in. "What happened?"

She was beyond holding back or being measured. She told him what had happened.

"Christ," said Drake. He shook his head.

She could see him pulling away from her. Was he going to abandon her too? That thought shook her heart, though she knew that it would be better for him to cut ties with her now. So far knowing her was the quickest route to death. Her hands started to shake.

Drake saw that and took them into his hands. "I'm sorry," he said, rubbing them. "We'll get him back. I promise."

She nodded her head, her shaking stopped. "If it is him."

"It has to be."

"There were many hims on that list of names I gave him."

"Very well. But you mentioned him earlier in the phone call. So it must have been him."

She wanted to believe it, but for some reason the phone call had crushed her confidence.

"Well. We have to act as if it's him."

She wanted to nod, but the tremors, which were building up in her fingers, spread, and suddenly she couldn't stop shaking.

Drake embraced her. "I'm sorry," he said.

"It's too dangerous," she said. "For anyone. We must stop." She could feel Drake shaking his head.

"It's okay," he said.

"You cannot do this. You will die."

"We'll die," he said.

"I meant soon."

He chuckled. "Death I'm not afraid of. He's a bastard, but I think I can face him down."

She shook again and suddenly tears started to stream down her cheek.

Drake hugged her, and she was glad that he hadn't walked away from her, though he had every reason to do so. She felt his warmth and hugged him tighter.

They ate dinner, and again she wondered why he didn't look at her, didn't observe her like she was used to so many men doing. For some reason that hurt, and again she wondered if perhaps he was just doing this for his parents' memory, or some other ideal, and that perhaps she was just a vehicle for him to achieve this. That thought filled her with cold, and though it made her uncomfortable, and distanced him from her, it at least was accompanied with numbness, and that was something precious to her right now.

When dinner was finished, Coral looked at Drake, who was still not casting his eyes her way.

"Thanks," she said. "That was great."

"You're welcome," he said. He cleared the plates. "Your phone's ringing," he said, pointing to the coat rack.

"What?" she said and pointed to her phone on the table in front of her. "Mine's right here."

"It's in your coat," he said and pointed again to the coat rack.

She looked and could see that indeed her coat pocket, from the coat she wore to the museum, had the outline of a phone's light. She walked over to it and pulled it out. It wasn't a phone she had ever seen before.

"Hello?" she answered.

"Hi."

It was a man.

"I'm sorry, who is this?"

"You don't know."

She wondered if it was a trick. But no trickster uses up a smartphone. Again a tremor spread through her body.

"It was the Texan."

"Excuse me?" she said.

"The Texan killed him."

"Who?" she asked, not entirely processing what was being said.

"Your father."

Her heart caved in. "Who is this?" she whispered.

"You won't know. Keep the phone."

The man hung up.

Drake came behind her and placed his hands on her shoulder. "Who was that?"

"A friend, I imagine," she said. But she knew that the world wasn't full of such characters and that she would have to be careful. "He said it was the Texan who killed."

"Who?" Drake said, his forehead furrowed.

"I don't know. It could be a trap."

Drake didn't answer. He returned to cleaning the dishes.

Coral stepped over to the information on the museum. So was it the Texan? Perhaps she didn't have time to be certain, but she felt more comfortable with placing all her energy behind robbing the man blind.

Someone knocked on the door and she startled.

It was Andy; he rushed in.

"What's wrong?" Drake asked.

"The security is the best I've ever seen," Andy said, shaking his head woefully.

"Even at night?" she asked.

"Especially at night," Andy said. "In fact I think the daytime is the only possibility."

"That's crazy," Drake said.

"No it isn't," Coral said. "I don't know how, but anything is possible. No security cordon is that tight."

"Okay, not impossible, but given our resources and time constraints, I would say impossible," Drake said.

Andy raised his finger. "But the daytime is the only time when they remove all but two security systems off."

"Which two?" asked Coral.

"Weight sensitive plates. The ones the artifacts rest on. And the too close motion sensors."

"And the men watching it at all times," Drake said.

133

"There are always men watching," said Andy.

They shared a tea, and after a few minutes, Andy left. "Too tired," he said to their pleas to stay.

When he was gone, Coral, somewhat happy, fell asleep on Drake's bed.

She woke up when Sophie started to meow in her ear.

"What is it?" she said, and the cat pranced back and forth between the kitchen and her. She walked up to a pile of cat food cans that the cat was sitting in front of. She glanced at her watch. She'd been sleeping in. She remembered the call from the previous night. A chill ran through her. Alexandros. Another chill ran through her. She opened a can for the cat and it started to eat away.

"Where's your owner at?" she asked the cat. Something in the apartment smelled wrong. Something outside the door seemed too still for a late morning in London.

She wanted to yell out Drake's name, to at least hear him, but a fear ran through her. It was silly, of course, but she felt like a child, thinking that her yelling might awake some monsters. No, she reminded her self, it wasn't that irrational. Her heart in her throat, she stepped towards Drake's bedroom. There was no one there.

"Drake?" she said softly. His room appeared to be more of a mess than before. But she wasn't certain. A suitcase, half packed, sat poking out of his closet. She checked the bathroom, and there was no one there either. Sophie, finished with her food, came by to rub her legs. Coral went back to the room and looked at the suitcase.

Was he thinking of leaving? Her heart dropped. Not that she would blame him. After all, things were getting much worse than even she'd ever expected. Again Alexandros' voice gurgled in her head. She sat down, her head spinning. So he was gone. The air felt heavy. And was that man who called someone trying to help, or another man trying to set a trap? She held her head between her knees. Things seemed to be spinning out of control. She was out of her element; she knew that. The wise choice was to cut her losses and bail. Tell Drake to bail. If he hadn't already.

She looked at the smallest pouch on the suitcase. It was opened with a photo hanging out. She pulled it and held it close. She took several deep breaths to calm herself down. The photo was Drake when he was younger, and two adults behind him. His parents, she assumed. They looked happy. A sharp pain went through her gut, spread to her chest and mind. He'd lost so much. She put the photo back and walked to the living room. She would have to figure out a way to get at the Texan. A daylight robbery in a museum full of people? Crazier things had been done before.

The doorknob started to jiggle. She started, looking around for a weapon. As the door opened, she grabbed a knife on the table in front of her.

"Easy," Drake said. "I come in peace."

His smile, and easy manner, both calmed and infuriated her.

"Where were you?" she asked, pointing the knife at him.

"I had a call from a friend. He found some information that will help us. A lot."

She searched his face. So he was staying. Her insides felt warm.

"Sorry I didn't tell you. I figured you needed the sleep."

She put down the knife and forced a sleep. Since when was she so volatile? "Sorry. I'm not usually like this."

"Of course. Some crazy things are happening. And," he said holding up a file full of papers. "There's a lot more that we didn't know about."

"Your friend?"

"I have a journalist friend. Best investigators in the world. Well, at least him."

"How's he holding up?" she asked.

"Oh, he's making it fine through the transition. Hell, he

even has a Twitter account with a hundred thousand followers."

"I meant with this investigation."

"Oh, that. Well, he's done more dangerous things for me before. He said it required a whole slew of new sources to get anything good on our Texan."

"Did you tell him to be careful?"

"He knows," Drake said.

She didn't want to risks someone else's life with this ordeal. "Drake."

"Don't worry, I told him about the trail of dead bodies. Don't worry. This guy has dealt with the CIA and the Chinese. He knows the risks."

She sat down at the table with him.

"Have you ever heard of a man named the Coyote?"

She tried to think of something since that name sounded familiar. "I think. I heard of him in certain circles. Ex-military. Maybe a mercenary."

Drake pointed at her. "Exactly. He is. A gun for hire, though lately it seems that the Texan has won over him."

"Oh?"

"That's right. He's his dog. And the intel chatter indicates that it's most likely that he was the one who killed..." Drake threw a grainy photo on the table. The man in it had sharp features with eyes that seemed to cut through the lens. "Apparently an hour after the photo was taken, the photographer died. Poisoned."

The man, seemed smart, and for some reason the photo made her tremble. She held it. So this was the man who killed her father.

"And he's here. In London," Drake added. "Looking, most likely for you. In fact, Interpol's also looking for you. And perhaps a few other agencies."

"Are you kidding me? Do they know—"

"Well, they all have this photo," Drake said and threw

another photo in front of her. She stared at the picture. It didn't seem to say much, but she was sure that they would be able to recognize her. How would she be able to operate outside of the apartment?

"So I got some supplies, to make you look more like a punk rocker than a respectable woman."

She raised her eyebrows. "Is that how you see me? As a respectable woman?" She was surprised to see Drake flush red.

"I was..." he said, as he held up a plastic bag from a drugstore.

She smiled and touched his elbow. She liked his skin. "I was kidding."

He glanced at her, holding a stare for a few seconds. She looked down when her heart started to beat too fast. "Anything else?" she said, shuffling her hand through the papers.

"That's it. If we see anyone who looks like this man, we'll find out. But I'm guessing, from how he's avoided detection so far, that he won't be easy to trace."

"If he's in London he might not have killed Alexandros," she said. "Maybe there's a team."

"We don't know where Alexandros was, do we?"

He was right. She had called a cell phone. Her heart started to beat fast, and her skin felt hot. "So we have to..." she trailed off, not knowing exactly what she was going to say about the assassin. She had a dangerous job, but mainly it involved staying in the shadows. And it never meant killing someone. She felt Drake's hand on hers. It calmed her, and she shook the picture of the Coyote. She was going to get him. If it was the last thing she did, she was going to get him.

"We will," Drake said.

She looked up at him. She wondered if he knew what she was thinking. "Thank you."

"But we have to locate him first."

Drake moved his seat closer to hers. "Maybe we can't do that. If he's such a ghost."

"I know how to be a ghost."

"Then we'll have to change that."

She cocked her head, not sure what he was trying to say.

"We'll have to bring him to us in a way we can control the situation."

"And how's that?"

"The museum. We'll get them there."

Coral noticed that Drake didn't say "get them" properly. He was scared about the killing. As was she. But she knew she had to do it. "I need a gun," she said.

"It will be hard, but I know some people in South Side London. They can help."

"Okay," she said. She knew how to shoot, so that wouldn't be the biggest issue. "But I also want to get something from the Texan. He must be taught a lesson," she said.

"I know," he said and chuckled.

"What's so funny?"

"It's him we should get."

"But the Coyote killed my father," she said.

"I know," he said and placed his hand on her shoulder, though he didn't seem to agree. "Do you know how you'll be able to steal from them in the day?"

She stared at the blueprints for a second. It was always best, when brainstorming how to rob a museum, to think of it like a story. When she could imagine herself there, she would be able to figure out where to go. "I think it's best to hit either near closing or opening."

"Dusk or dawn sort of thing?"

"Exactly," she said. "I'd say closing. We know where the generators are. We have to hit those."

"Aren't there emergency lights?"

"For exits. There's nothing bright. Not with the system

they have installed. It's the best we can do."

"What do we hit it with?" said Drake.

That was the hard part. Father was always the one to help her with logistics.

"We need someone there to hack away at the wires. But at the end of the day, it would be better to have a small charge placed that we can detonate whenever we need to."

"But isn't that risky? It's in the basement, and the signal might not reach it."

She waved him away with her hand. "We have a timer as backup," she said, noticing that her dismissal slightly perturbed him, but she had no time for pleasantries, her mind was ticking away.

"What about explosives," he said. "I know I can't get that."

"I had an old boyfriend at Hereford. He might be able to help."

That really seemed to suck the blood out of Drake's face. She couldn't help but grin.

"Very well. Then how do we get past the security guards? There were too many, even in the day. And even if you get past them, how will you get past the security on each case. They're all battery-backed."

"I know," she said, drumming her fingers on the table. She imagined the security guards, some mercenaries, all staring at the artifacts. And what would they do once the lights went dim? They would adjust. But not unless it happened too quickly. And not unless they were distracted. But how? "Do you know any homeless people?" she said.

"No. Not really. Well, maybe a couple. Well, let's get to know more than a couple."

"Why's that?"

Her mind, already on the next thing, slowed down, she didn't like this. "Some homeless men are used by the police to keep an eye on the streets. You need to use your contacts your journalist friend has with the police to make sure that we're not dealing with one of theirs."

"How—"

"Just say you're trying to do a story on homeless rights or something. But once that's done, we'll have to recruit a at least twenty."

"You'll see," she said with a grin.

"And where do you plan to be when this happens? I mean, how do we get the items out?"

"I'm not a hundred percent on it, but I thing the vents are the only way."

"Are you sure?" Drake said. "Andy said that those were mined with motion sensors too."

"But those were based on the main system. And once we cut the main system and the generator, we'll be golden."

She stood up full of energy. Before Drake could say anything she was outside, giving a call to her ex, a crazy sniper who used to be in the SAS.

She met him in a town a few stops away from Hereford. It was a gray town with green grass everywhere, and a slowness to it that seemed to be almost forced. The ex seemed the same. Shaggy hair and eyes that smiled then cut into you. She still liked the way his shirt and pants outlined his muscles, but she remembered how odd he was. And how much she hated talking to him. But he was nice, at the end of the day, and he merely grinned when she told him what she wanted. He led her to a warehouse near an abandoned farm and handed her the keys.

"Tell me you're not going to blow up the Underground, are you?"

"Don't be silly," she replied.

"I mean it. I remember how rebellious you were."

"And I remember how much you loved the Crown," she snapped back.

He laughed. "Always the wild one."

Her body twitched. Memories of times in bed spent with him. She stared at the explosives as he went over how to place a charge and detonate it. There wasn't much, perhaps a pound's worth of C4, but it was enough. She liked being in his presence. In knowing that she had a pit bull on her side.

"You in trouble?" he asked.

"What do you mean?" she asked.

"Come on. You're going to lie? You weren't all that good at that. Even when you were getting information from me," he said and flashed that easy smile again.

"I might be," she said. "But don't worry about it."

"I didn't say I was," he said, observing her.

She felt his steel eyes lick her. She didn't mind it. "You ever heard of the Coyote?"

He whistled. "That's who's after you? Christ, Coral. What *have* you done?"

"I did what was right."

"What's right is wrong if it gets you killed."

"So much for Mr. Crown's loyalty."

He laughed. "You have someone else helping you?" he asked.

"I do."

"He got a good head?"

She wondered how he knew. "He does."

"Good," he said. "If you're in a jam give me a call," he said.

She knew he rarely gave out such assurances. In fact it was one of the things she'd hated about him. Her lower lip quivered. "I just might," she said.

"He's an ornery bastard."

"Who?"

"Coyote. American SOF. He was never anything but a prick when I saw him."

"You've worked with him?"

"Only partially. He left and became a merc. He's good,

141

but he's human. Don't forget that."

"Any weaknesses?" she asked.

"Hard to say," he said. He scratched his chin and looked off into the distance. "There was a confidence about him that was misplaced. In other words, if he thinks he has you on the ropes he goes in because he expects that and assumes he's that good. He *is* good. But no one's as good as he thinks he is. He's just been lucky."

"Any tips on how to make him less lucky?"

"Just do as I said. Make him think he's got you. Then snap back. You still a good shot?"

"I was taught by the best," she said. He'd spent hours teaching her how to hone her shooting skills. Back then she'd only piled it on to the things that made him crazy, but now she could see how good he'd been to her.

He smiled. It seemed sad.

She returned to London late at night. Drake was waiting on the sofa.

"I have the gun," he said.

She could tell right away that his voice was lower, and that he seemed larger somehow.

"Thank you," she said. "I'll take your word that it fires."

"Any luck?" he asked.

Yes, his voice was definitely gruff. She couldn't help but grin.

"I got a few things," she said and held up a bag full of explosives. She saw his eyes widen. "Don't worry, I've handled them before," she said. "We'll be able to cut the wires. And I've kept the charges and the explosives apart. Let's hope Sophie doesn't go eating messing with it."

He glared at Sophie. "You hear that?" The cat meowed.

Coral plopped down next to Drake. "And the homeless people?"

Taj and Andy are on that.

Feeling calm, she took his hand. He seemed surprised.

"What next?" he said.

"Weren't you going to make me a punk rocker?"

He nodded. He led her to the bathroom. She let him cut her hair short. She felt his hands on her head, lulling her into a numbness.

"You've done this before?" she said.

"Nope," he said.

He bleached her hair, and let it sit, while he pulled out some tight black jeans and get up that reminded Coral of her times in college. But they looked like they would be completely different. "Do you think I can look that young?" she asked.

"Of course," he said. He then dyed her hair indigo blue. She stared at the person in front of her. It was so different already. That's when he pulled out the needle.

"What's that for?" she asked.

"You want to be a punk rocker, right?"

She stared at it. "Do you know what you're doing?"

"Of course," he said. "I Googled it."

"Are you kidding me?" she said.

"Yeah. I've done this before. Used to be a little of a punk rocker myself."

She tried to discern if there was some punchline, but he appeared serious. She watched as he applied some antiseptic to her ear, then the needle. The searing pain that followed almost blinded her. He did three holes in the upper part of each ear. Then one in each nose. Then one in each eyebrow.

"How big is that needle?" she asked.

"The only size a punk rocker would be seen with."

She narrowed her eyes at him. He seemed to be enjoying himself.

"You know you might need some needles too."

He laughed. She really liked his laugh.

"Come on, one more for the tongue."

"You're kidding me."

"I'm telling you, if you don't have one on the tongue they're going to wonder."

She agreed after staring him down for a minute. "All right," she said. "Let's try."

He numbed her tongue with some Lydocain, then pulled out a new needle for her tongue.

"If it gets infected, or anything, I'm going to castrate you."

He seemed nervous.

When it had gone through and he placed a stud in each hole, she lay in his bed going over the tongue stud between her teeth. She didn't have a long time to plan the museum heist. They'd gone over the basic plan. But they would soon need a detailed one. One that included killing the Coyote. She remembered her ex's reaction. That hadn't been good. Her ex was a bold man, but even he had paused when Coyote's name was mentioned.

She heard Drake come in.

"Sophie wants to stay with you."

She didn't reply.

"I'm sorry, but it's a good getup. They'll never think twice," he said.

She rolled her eyes.

"You don't think so?" he said.

"No. It's a good idea." She knew *she* didn't recognize the person on the other side of the mirror. That was surely a good thing.

She fell asleep. Her last thoughts were on the way Drake smiled. She felt warm inside, but that went away as she thought of the phone call from Alexandros. She had to assume he was dead. And if he was, what was she to do? The room started suffocating her.

She woke up, sweating, the sounds of horns in the distance. A creak sent her flying up.

"Drake?"

"Sorry about that," Drake said.

She could barely see his outline at the doorway.

"Is everything all right?" she asked. Her heart was beating fast, though she was sure it wasn't because she was scared. She trusted Drake. Or did she? She tried to discern if anything was in his hands. He walked up to her bed.

"I couldn't sleep either. Then I heard you. You were having a nightmare," he said. "You mentioned Alexandros."

"My father's friend."

"On the phone," Drake said.

Coral, still trying to make out what was going on, could feel the warmth of Drake's skin even though he stood more than a meter from her. She also felt her heart beating faster than ever. But now that she was certain it wasn't fear she could feel the ends of her limbs start to tingle. She willed him to sit next to her, but she didn't say anything.

"Do you mind?" he said.

She nodded, hoping that he could see her movement. He sat down next to her, and she could smell his musk.

"It's a scary situation when you think about it," he said.

"It is," she said.

"But we're going to get them."

"I know." She didn't say anything about the possibility that it might not work. Instead, she held her breath, certain that he could hear her heart. She felt his hand on hers. Her heart stopped, then continued to beat fast. She could feel that neither of them wanted to talk about failure. How this powerful force they were facing was very easily going to defeat them. How it was going to crush them and rejoice in their blood and if not, it would most certainly tarnish both their reputations beyond repair and history would remember them as nothing but foolish rebels. She knew that, and knew he knew it, but wanted to forget it because they were going to step forward to confront the machine anyways.

145

He rubbed her hand for a few seconds.

"I'm going to have to kiss you."

She almost smiled, but didn't. She could feel his lips brush against hers, hesitate, then touched. Her skin burned and she floated.

She kissed back. Her breathing deepened, and she could feel his hands on her face, and then on her hips. He didn't move further.

It seemed like an eternity before her heart slowed to a steady, though still fast, beat. Her skin burned. She ran her hands over his body, the sharp hard angles were perfect places to rest her hands. He kissed her all over her face, then her neck.

He undid her blouse. And pants. She undid his shirt, barely making out his outline in the dark.

His mouth moved down her, and she could feel a tender splash of pleasure.

She felt him, and she guided him into her mouth, then between her legs.

He was on top of her, and he slowly pushed inside her. He slowed down, kissing her, and she guided his hips before getting on top of him. She could feel a melting of her soul. He grabbed her and held her tight, whispering something she couldn't quite make out, though it sounded foreign to her.

Over and over, until she felt him shudder inside her, his hands clenching her shoulders until it was painful.

She fell asleep on his chest.

When she woke up in the morning, she saw that Drake was talking in the living room. It was afternoon again, and she didn't know why that bothered her.

"Good news," Drake said. "They have fifteen homeless guys more than willing to do as we need."

"None are cops?"

"I'm running the names, but we should be good."

There was a pause. He touched her hair. And just then her

phone started to ring again, the phone that wasn't hers. She answered it, annoyed that she was being prevented from talking to Drake.

"Yes?" she said.

"Are you still in your flat?"

She paused, wondering if she should say anything to confirm that.

The man on the other side sighed, exasperated. "Listen. They know where you are. Take what you can and get out. You haven't but a minute, you got me?"

Before she could say anything, the man hung up.

"What?" Drake asked.

"It was the same man. He said that they're coming."

"Now?"

She nodded, feeling light-headed.

"Well, let's get out. I know a back way."

"What if it's a joke?"

"Then it's good practice," he said.

Energy rushed through her body; she ran to the table and started to scoop up all the planning papers and papers on the museum.

"Take your clothes and explosives," he said, pointing at a large empty backpack.

A siren sounded in the distance. Coral could feel her chest expanding and her vision narrowing. The sirens grew louder.

She moved to the explosives, and she saw him with two bags, pulling her out of the door.

"Sophie?" she asked.

"She's in here," he said, pointing at a carrying bag.

She lifted her backpack, not sure if that was everything. But the sirens were louder, then suddenly they cut off. They were in the hallway, but moving away from the front door. She looked back. Everything seemed quiet. There was a whining sound in her ear. She could hear a pipe dripping, and she wanted to sleep.

Aaron Grunn

But the sound of boots on the floor above pushed blood into her legs, and she followed Drake into the boiler-room. He kicked open a door. There was only the sound of a furnace now. Though Coral wasn't sure why it was so loud. They entered a small dank room, the smell of cold concrete everywhere, and down stairs. Then up a ladder. Drake leaned into a door and opened it slowly. Coral froze when she saw the policeman standing right in front of them.

Matt woke up, his phone ringing. For a second he reached over and hoped that Kim had returned, but she hadn't. He felt his heart moan again.

"Yes" he said.

"Are you ready?" It was Kim.

"Sure," he said, looking down at his wrinkled clothes.

"Get down to the lobby."

He could hear cars outside and for a second he wasn't sure where he was. But he put on his clothes, and by the time he was in the hallway, he felt sad because he knew where he was. And he also thought about the only reason Kim could be calling him: she had found the thief. That was something Matt could have done without, but he was beyond that, and he needed to do his job.

He stepped into the elevator and jumped back when he saw Coyote. The man was stooped, though, as if he was tired.

"What's wrong, Matt? A little rough today, aren't we?"

Matt composed himself and stepped into the elevator, reminding himself that the Coyote could smell fear. As the door closed, and Matt could see from the corner of his eye that the camera had been sprayed over with black paint, his legs wobbled. He wouldn't put it past Coyote to shoot him right there and then. Had he found out his true reason? How?

"That Korean is a tasty treat," Coyote said.

"I didn't know you were into that."

Coyote puffed his chest out. "What do you mean?"

"Always took you for a smoker, if you know what I mean?"

"Oh?" Coyote said, leaning back and laughing. "Is that because you always fall for your women, let them drag you down, while I don't? And I have the better career than you?"

Matt shrugged. "What business is it of yours?"

Coyote raised his eyebrows. "Now we're proper. Letting this London air get to your head, aren't you?"

Matt took a second to square up to Coyote. He could

sense something off about the man. "You having problems finding the woman, aren't you? And now you want me to help you find her. Is that right?"

Coyote seemed to flinch before an ominous grin spread across his face, and the shadow of his nose fell on his teeth like a wave.

"I know who the woman is, Matt," Coyote said. "And I hope you know that your job is in jeopardy if this woman somehow manages to escape. So why not just tell me?"

Matt felt his face growing hot. "Did the Texan tell you that? As you were eating out of the palm of his hand? Or was it after he fucked you from behind?"

Coyote stepped forward. "Don't talk down to me you washed up operator. You would die to have the payments I do. And yes, the Texan told me to send him a list of anyone who stands in my way. That scare you? I hope it does, because there'll be no life for you to live if you do decide to cross me."

Matt felt his throat tighten, because he knew that he was on thin ice as it was, and Coyote probably did have the Texan's ear.

"I'll throw some scraps your way when I get them," Matt said.

The elevator door opened, and he turned into the lobby. He could see Kim standing outside. Her face was stolid, as if he were a stranger. Could she be *that* cold? He turned to say something to Coyote, but he was gone. He looked around, but there was no sign of him. He was good, Coyote, and Matt would have to watch his step, because he didn't need the man to become rabid.

"Hi," Matt said stepping up to Kim. He wanted to hug her, but the look in her eye was fierce. "How are you?" he asked, trying to be proper.

"I'm fine," she said, opening the backdoor of the limo. "Please."

"This is very nerve-wracking, you know?" Matt said,

trying to lighten things up. He didn't want to sound pathetic, but he wanted a hint of the affection from the previous night. "Do I have to wear a blindfold?"

"Maybe," she said. Her face was still hard. It was difficult to see the same woman who'd been in his arms the previous night. As he stepped by her, he felt her hand brush against his crotch. He looked at her, but she was looking off into the street, her lips cracked into a smirk. Matt felt his blood pressure rise, and as he sat down on the other side of the car, he could feel himself rising in his seat. She sat down next to him.

"So what's the deal?" he said.

"You're being followed," she said, looking ahead at the driver as they merged into traffic.

"What do you mean—Oh Coyote? Well, nothing we can do about him." Her smell reminded him of last night and he tried to appear as nonchalant as he could.

The car drove a few blocks then stopped at a stoplight. The driver had a thick brown neck, though Matt couldn't see anything other characteristics. The driver was silent enough that Matt knew he was listening.

"So where are we going?" Matt said.

"Our headquarters. I'll show you what we have."

They parked in front of a non-descript gray office building that reached five stories. But Matt could tell the difference, if the civilian pedestrians who walked by couldn't. He could see the extra cameras and the plainclothes agents on the corner who seemed a little too observant. He stepped out of the car and up to the front door, which Kim held for him.

They walked into a lobby. A man with a submachine gun watched them. Kim stepped in front of a kiosk and placed her hand on a scanner. Then her eyes in front of a camera hole.

"Thank you," said the svelte female voice.

"Thank you," Kim said. A beep sounded. Kim typed a few things into the kiosk and ushered Matt in front.

He could see a screen that said guest. He placed his palm and had his retina scanned.

"Thank you," said the robot.

"Thank you," said Matt.

After a few seconds in an elevator they came up to an open floor. "Nice," said Matt.

Kim glanced at him. "I'm sure I don't have to tell you that you can't mention this to anyone."

"Of course," said Matt. "I was just going to say that your security is impressive."

She looked at him. He caught a glint in her eye that made his stomach churn. Was she that much in control of him?

She guided him to an office and he walked in. He felt tired and rubbed his eyes, grime still in the edges.

"Coffee?" she asked and walked over to a coffee-capsule machine. As the machine ground out a coffee, and beautiful rich corresponding aromas, Matt examined the room, and when he could, her curves. The room consisted of a desk and a table. But unlike almost every office he had ever been in, nothing hung on the walls, and nothing, besides a computer and the coffee machine, on the desk. The carpet, typical of all new office buildings, was short-haired, dark purple and without a single stain.

He downed the coffee, something dark. "You like dark?" he said, noticing that she hadn't asked about milk or sugar.

She eyed him without replying as she drank her cup.

He suppressed a smirk thinking about the "I'm sweet enough" line he used when asked for sugar, as he pictured her using it. When he was finished, he placed his cup next to the coffee machine. "This isn't your place, is it?"

She placed down her half-finished cup. "No."

That she was being extremely unhelpful was annoying him. "So there's no news on the woman?"

"I told you. I'm just showing you around."

"Is there a team?" he said. He knew he should've been

more patient, but he couldn't help it. Her actions, her pure apathy towards him was infuriating.

"Yes."

He opened his mouth to say something, but she raised her finger and answered her phone.

After a few okays she hung up.

"We got her," she said.

Her smile, so victorious, made Matt feel sick.

"You do?" he said, noticing that he was losing his own voice. His armpits grew wet.

She pulled out a gun and made sure it was loaded. Matt felt small in front of her, and he tried to will the woman from last night to come out.

"She's been caught?" he asked.

"No. We have her position. You can come," she said as she hurried out of the room.

"Good," he said. His skull tightened around his brain. He could barely think. "Let me use the bathroom."

She glanced back at him, with an icy look. She pointed to a bathroom.

He rushed in.

When he came out she was looking at him and her watch.

He started to apologize but she just grabbed his wrist and took off in a fast jog down the hallway. Her touch, cold, and everything about her was hard and hateful. Instead of taking her cue and being professional, he felt jilted. Like a fool.

He jumped into the back of the same limo.

"We have to catch up," said the thick-necked driver. His accent was Pacific, but Matt couldn't place where. Maori, if he had to guess. He craned his neck to look for a tattoo.

Kim tapped him. He looked over and saw playfulness in her eyes.

"You took your time, didn't you?"

He wasn't sure if she was teasing him or angry. He could smell her perfume, and underneath that her sweat. His heart moved. She looked away as if he disgusted her. "Turn here, it'll be easier to catch up."

The wheels of the car squealed and after the engine revved and they turned again, the driver showing his skills by pulling the hand brake and power sliding into a perpendicular street, they found themselves behind two black armored cars.

"So how did you find her?" Matt said.

"Cell phone records. And we saw someone like her in the museum."

Matt's heart jumped. "No."

"Yes," she said, looking at the armored cars ahead. "Do we have to ride like an army every time? Didn't I ask for undercover carriers?"

"I know miss," said the driver. "Boss wasn't having any of it."

"Why not? We have enough in the budget for it."

"Yeah, but this is what the politicians want to see."

Matt chuckled to himself. It's what was wanted in the states too. One couldn't have too subtle of an intel unit anymore or else no one would notice and being noticed these days was one of the best forms of recruiting and advertising and getting more money for more of the same.

Kim glared at him.

They drove to a less crowded part of London, where there were more leaves. There were a few houses with tiled roofs and Matt stared at people with shopping bags; his beating heart had calmed and smelling Kim, he felt domestic for the first time in a long time and he wondered where, if anything ever worked out between them, they would choose to live. He even fancied asking her, but knew he was truly being foolish now.

"We're almost there," said Kim.

Matt nodded, trying to seem calm. He used to be the one who ran into the houses. Not anymore. He was now a man outside looking in. He always wondered how the citizens of any nation allowed their police to kick down doors with such impunity. Especially in such a peaceful town.

"You all right?" Kim asked.

"I've done this before," he retorted. He really didn't like it when she acted like this. He watched as men poured out of the armored trucks in front of them. Some policemen were helping to cordon off the neighborhood. He stepped out. The chilly but clean air helped him calm down. But he still felt helpless about what was going to happen next.

Kim seemed so excited at the prospect of catching the thief that he hated her. The driver, also out of the car looked him over. Matt could definitely see a tattoo creeping up his neck. The man grinned at him as if there was a joke between them. He pulled out a pack of cigarettes and tilted his head at Matt.

"Sure," said Matt, and the man popped a cigarette out. They lit up and Matt drew in the smoke. He sucked in hard, hoping that it would hurt him, hoping that a cell would go cancerous, because he was feeling too helpless otherwise. He watched as the men stormed into the front door. A ladder led up to the roof and a few stormed up that way too. Same tactics everywhere, thought Matt.

"You like this?" the driver asked.

Matt could sense a violence about the man. Something more than the size of his lats. Like he'd been on the wrong side of the law before. His movements, the darting and laser-like focus of his eyes.

"No," said Matt. He knew about the connotations that such a manly activity, breaking down a door and overwhelming someone with superior numbers and weapons, always brought up. In his experience, only women were allowed to complain. And yet it seemed like Kim relished this. "You?"

"Don't care for any of this, really."

"But?"

"But it's a paycheck, right?"

A window shattered in the distance. Someone screamed. "That it is. Where you from?" asked Matt. He wanted to know something about this man in front of him.

"Auckland. North of. You?"

"New York," said Matt.

The driver stared ahead and clucked while shaking his head. "They did this in my community. You know how they think about drugs."

Matt didn't know why the Maori was including him in hating on "they" but he liked it. "Any excuse for a war."

The Maori clucked and shook his head. "You know who they're catching?"

"Yeah, you?"

"Yup," the Maori said and sucked in a huge lungful of smoke and billowed it into the air. Matt noticed a vein in his neck throb. So the man wasn't some low level driver. Not if he knew what was going on.

"Another good person dragged down into the earth," said the driver.

Matt's heart lifted slightly. "That's the way it goes. Always." He too sucked down on his cigarette. Kim was barking something down a radio.

"What about her?" Matt asked.

"She's good people. But a girl scout. Not sure if she'll ever see the bigger picture."

Matt looked over at Kim's jawline. He felt a deep concern for her. "That's good. At least she'll live a prosperous life."

The driver nodded and took another drag when a flash bang went off and blew out a window. "Christ. Like storm troopers. Always."

Matt nodded. "I know."

"Well at least one good person will survive," said the driver as he nodded over to Kim. Then he stared at Matt.

Matt felt heat creeping up his torso. He wasn't certain

what the driver meant. "Well..." he said and took another hit of nicotine. Then he realized what the Maori was trying to say. That Matt had been hoping to bring Kim into his worldview, but he shouldn't have. That in fact he should leave her be. But didn't she come to him? Looking at her barking orders down the radio, he wasn't sure. He felt lonely, and he threw his cigarette into a oily puddle near a gutter.

"It'll be fine," said the driver.

"How's that?" asked Matt.

The driver shrugged, then grinned.

"Let's go," Kim said. They've cleared it."

"Is she contained?"

Kim marched towards the front door.

Matt trotted to keep up with her. "Did they..."

He found himself in a dark apartment that seemed sad more than anything.

"We found nothing," the leader of the troops said.

Kim nodded, annoyed, and kicked over a bowl of cat food.

"They were just here," said Kim.

"How do you know?" Matt asked. He stepped aside to allow some of the other men to take samples of everything in the apartment.

"They took all their information."

"Maybe they're just out for the day," said Matt.

"No. They heard us," Kim said, flashing an angry look at the head of the troops. The man must have worked with Kim before because he rolled his eyes.

"How do you know?" Matt asked Kim again.

"Where's their cat? Who takes their cat?"

Matt felt a stab in his gut. He wondered how far Kim was going to follow this thread. "Still..." was all he could manage to say.

"No way they heard us. I'm guessing they were tipped off," said the head of the troops.

Matt felt the man stare at him, so he looked up and eyeballed the man back.

"Right," Kim said and started to search through the closet.

"We can plant devices in the hope they'll be back," said Matt.

"We could," said Kim. She seemed to pull herself together. "We will. It's SOP."

Matt could feel the driver move next to him.

"Damn shame," said the driver.

"That it is," said Matt. He could feel the driver burning a hole in his neck. He headed out for some fresh air.

He heard small footsteps follow him.

"If you want I can have him drive you back, since there's nothing to see here."

Matt turned and looked at Kim. So cold. He didn't like that. Didn't like that she had an iron grip on his heart, and could turn up or off the heat at a whim.

"That won't be necessary," he said and turned and walked away.

The neighborhood seemed perfect if someone wanted peace. The neighbors were staring as if they hadn't seen something like this in ages. Funny thing to think about how much London had been through, more than New York, and still have coddled masses. Still, if he was going to stay someplace it would be in a dirtier part of town. A place where people despised the police and their heavy-handed ways.

He walked past a police cordon and wondered if he was ever going to see this woman again.

He found a taxi, though he ended up heading to the museum and talking to the security there. No one seemed perturbed, as there hadn't been any notable acts for the day. The security systems were all tip top as well. He wondered if Kim had enough evidence to show that the thief had truly been tipped off. He got a call from Tim who hinted that they'd managed to get friends in the NSA to comb through London's entire cell phone registry to find hints of a word that a thief might use. Matt wished him luck.

That's when he saw Coyote. At first Matt felt like ducking and leaving, but he decided that he needed the madman on his side. Or at least less testy.

"Hey!" Matt said.

Coyote slithered over. "Well, look at what the cat dragged in."

"We barely missed her," Matt said.

"I know," Coyote said, smiling too broadly for Matt's tastes.

"Nothing found."

"Most likely tipped off," said Coyote.

"Or the tanks we rolled in with tipped them off."

Coyote observed Matt's face with such intensity that Matt's feet shifted.

"Looks like we missed our chance," said Matt.

"You're a funny one," Coyote said. There was a hint of affection in his voice. Matt didn't know what to do with that.

"Why's that?"

"You're helping me now."

"Apparently you have my bosses' balls."

Coyote clucked. "The ever loyal Matt."

"Come on," said Matt. "You going to put up this show forever?"

Coyote clucked again. "Where's your girlfriend?"

"Not mine... Let's stay focused on the task at hand."

"Uh oh. She dump you already? I'm sorry. What's wrong?" Coyote's hand reached out and tapped Matt's groin. "Not working eh? Age's a cruel prankster."

"Fuck off," said Matt, swinging at, and missing, Coyote's arm.

Coyote chuckled. "Well, if you can't do the business, I

159

suppose it's back to business."

"That it is." Matt didn't know why he was turning red. "We might have missed our chance."

Again Coyote was observing him.

"You find out anything of use?" Matt asked.

"You think we've missed our chance?"

"Especially after this caper," Matt said.

"Why didn't you tell me as it was happening?" Coyote said.

"No time. We were told and I'd to head out."

Coyote didn't seem to believe him. "Because if you wanted to help, that would have gotten rid of this nuisance quicker than ever."

"Well, there was no time," said Matt. "What next is what matters."

"Let's get one thing straight. That isn't what matters. I think you're full of shit, on top of being impotent. Give me some information that's valuable and I'll do the same."

"What do we do if she's flown the coop?" Matt asked, hating Coyote with every single bone in his body.

"She hasn't. She's here for revenge which makes her completely vulnerable."

Before Matt could add anything else, Coyote turned and marched away.

Matt spent the rest of the day going over the museum's security. When he was done he headed to his hotel room, hungry, but too tired to eat out again. And he felt lonely. Being amongst the throngs would only make that worse.

A knock on his door woke him up from a dream.

It was raining outside. He wondered if Coyote was back to torment him.

He opened the door, half hoping for a bullet to end his misery. But there she was, Kim, looking at him with her head tilted. His heart spiked into his brain, and he stepped aside.

She brushed past him, but he was thinking about what the driver said, so though he received a rush of blood through his groin, it died down as he felt that they weren't meant to be. She sat on his bed and looked at him, her head still tilted.

"You look rough," she said.

He sat down, a few feet away from her. He could smell her sweat and it enticed him to smile. He quickly suppressed it.

"I'm fine. Was anything else found?" he asked.

"Nothing. I'm certain that they were either tipped off by the loud tanks that we followed, or more likely, they were tipped off by someone else."

Matt felt his heart beat fast again, then moan and fall weak in his chest. Perhaps he was getting too old for all this. He felt her eyes searching him. He welcomed it, but when it made him feel uncomfortable he lay back on the bed, staring at the ceiling. He was too tired to fight off any tells that may have been showing on his face.

"So you think you have a mole?" he asked. Luckily, his voice didn't crack.

"That's a possibility." She stood up. "My boss thinks it's the driver. He's been one to make odd comments every now and then."

"I don't think it's him," said Matt. He liked the driver and didn't want anything to happen to him.

"Maybe. But it's always good to check up. My boss was wondering if you could send up all his electronic data."

Matt paused. "You have—"

"Here," she said and handed him a sheet with phone numbers and IP addresses.

"I'll call my boss and have him look into it," he said. Though he felt sorry for the driver, he also experienced a cool relief come over him.

"What exactly did the driver say?" he asked.

"I've heard him talk about the foolishness of what we do.

Of what we all do."

There was actual hurt in her voice. Matt felt himself pull further and further away from her. She seemed so foreign, and for a second he felt so alone that his body shrank beyond all logic.

"That is horrid," he said, not able to dress the ironic tone that he felt towards her now.

She cocked her head at him. Then she tsked. "What is life to you, Matt?"

"What?"

"You heard me."

"We were talking about the driver."

"I know," she said.

"Are you..." He thought better of what he'd to say. He thought of the driver, and he thought of the thief, and of the fact that this beautiful woman in front of him was nothing more than a shell. Then he thought himself unfair. Anger and sadness rolled into a ball and choked him. "Life is what it is," he said.

He looked into her eyes and watched as she observed him with a cruelty fitting of someone in their line of work.

"Why do you work where you do?" she asked.

"I don't have much of a choice, do I?" he said. "It's either that or starve and watch my parents starve."

"That's the way it's always been. Don't think yourself special."

He sat up and looked at her. "So the driver shouldn't be afforded any level of privacy just because of a few thoughts of his."

"Words, not thoughts. Thoughts people can keep."

Matt shook his head. "Christ."

"What? You think you're smarter than the people you're scoffing?"

"Maybe not."

"Then why claim to know more?"

"I'm not," Matt said, annoyed that she seemed to be entering his thoughts. "I didn't say anything."

"You're protecting the driver."

"Because..." He tried to think of something, but realized that perhaps she was right: that the situation was too complex for him to ever encapsulate at one time in his head so perhaps he should forget it. But his body wouldn't allow it, and it rebelled when he tried to, in his head, make nice with her. "So you think it's fine to watch a man for words? To formulate how to end his life?"

"He's a suspect. He shouldn't say things that weaken the team he's playing for."

"His choice is to be chased by our kind till the end of his days, or not. And that's about it."

"That's not true."

A silence enveloped Matt. He heard cars outside, felt bitter about the world going about its business without caring for the consequences of its waste.

"What do you think about *your* job?" Matt asked.

"It's necessary. Do you think the world would be better without us?"

"I never said that."

"Don't tell me you're broke," she said.

The jab cracked his heart, and he felt nothing for her. Even the anger dissolved into a numbness. "What?"

"You were military. I read. So was Coyote. And now you're no more than a broken tool."

He stared at her. The rising and falling of his chest seemed to expand and contract the room. Everything but her grew darker, and he felt further removed from her and the bustling world outside.

"That's what you think?" he asked. He felt like admitting everything, but then decided to hold out from her forever.

"No," she said. "I just wanted to see your reaction."

"Perhaps you're right."

163

"I'm not," she said softly.

"I'm the broken tool, unfit for the machine. Right? And you, so well tread and oiled. All you want is to catch this evil thief, right?"

She shook her head and stepped towards him. "I was just—"

"Testing me? Answer the question." He could feel his head light, his voice turning into a growl, blood rushing past his thighs and ears. She flinched a fraction of an inch, and he didn't care.

"I didn't mean to."

"I'm talking about the thief," he said.

"She's causing bloodshed; surely you see this? There are other methods to what she's doing," she said.

He stared at her, her hands reached over to his shoulders, and he felt the room all dark but her face. His hands moved, without his permission, to her hips. He wasn't himself, and he wasn't sure what was going on. He could feel her tremble, and could feel the warmth of her breath near his lips.

He kissed her. Slowly her skin became bare, goose-bumped, and he could smell her in his blood. The next few moments were a blur of a nipple pressed by his chest. A gasp of hers in his ear. A thigh. A long moan. A glimpse of her curve, and the rush. Before she arched and writhed. Before he shuddered and felt her wet skin on his. He closed his eyes, thinking of nothing.

The room consisted of a bed and a cupboard. It had a half window to watch the calves of London's worker bees scurrying along. Taj had found them this place. A cousin of his hadn't been able to rent it out. Coral could see why. The sink in the bathroom leaked brown water, and the shower was filled with mold. Between the walls she could hear the scurrying of creatures of some kind, but she didn't dare peek through the cracks. She'd been awake for sometime now, while Drake slept beside her. He was still, so peaceful, that though she wanted to talk to him, she didn't want to disturb his rest.

The shouting of two men echoed in the room. A couple next doors having a fight. A door slammed. Then again. The shouting shifted to the hallway. The two men seemed about to kill each other. She thought of her father and Alexandros; she wondered how they fought, if ever. And she realized that she'd never fully pictured a gay couple's fight. Jilted lovers. Jealousy. Betrayal. Surely that was the ultimate violence between two people? After all, with the proverbial nothing to lose, and nothing but testosterone, wouldn't it all end violently? But she hadn't heard of too many such fights or murders.

A body slammed against the hallway wall. She contained herself from walking out. Some more yelling followed by complete silence.

She could feel her heart beating. It slowed down. She was cold, and she moved in closer to Drake. He murmured and smiled at something in his dream. Someone in the building opened a tap and the pipes moaned. She was tired, but couldn't sleep. A door slammed. She thought about what they'd to do next. They needed a perfectly formulated plan.

Last night they'd talked to Andy in hushed whispers. The thought of getting caught didn't frighten the two old men. In fact it seemed to fill them with energy.

And still she couldn't shake off the feeling that she was being suffocated by a being that only existed in every surface of the earth and in the air. She wondered why she thought she could avoid the same fate that those who had taught her everything she knew, had in fact been better at everything than she, had themselves met. And that hope that she'd come out on top evaporated, and suddenly her insides felt tight, her throat collapsed. The smell of the room, bleach and cement, filled her nostrils and she felt sick.

"You look rough," said Drake.

She relaxed. "I'm fine. We need to get going," she said, trying to sound angry, though she was glad he was up.

"Why? Andy needs to contact us first, doesn't he?"

She sighed.

"They got lucky," he said. "Don't worry, we're good. We'll stay off phones for now."

"I have a horrid feeling," she said and rubbed her stomach. I think that everyone I know will die."

"We won't," he said, moving in and hugging her. "I promise."

"You can't promise that."

"It'll be fine," he said.

And though she felt patronized, and knew he couldn't possibly be basing his words on fact, she decided to believe him.

They ate breakfast out of a pre-made meal in the small refrigerator in the only closet which smelled like damp brick. The meal, crackers and cheese and salami, were stale, dry. But she was hungry enough that it didn't matter. Gone were the days that she would enjoy the finer things in life; she was sure of this.

A knock sounded on the door. Drake answered it with a handgun in hand. Andy and Taj walked in, both of them beaming.

"Everything's in place," Andy said, beaming. "We're ready for your orders, ma'am."

Coral felt everyone staring at her. She couldn't possibly

imagine what to do next. Her mind went blank.

"Sit down," Drake said.

Coral wasn't certain who he was talking to, or where they were going to sit.

She felt Andy's hand on her shoulder.

"I don't know," she said. "I don't want anyone to get hurt."

"Nonsense," Taj said. "We're soldiers, and we know what we're doing." He hit his chest with his hand. It sounded brittle.

"I have a bad feeling. Stronger than I've ever felt before."

"What?" Drake asked.

"I have the feeling that we're being toyed with. That the man who called just wanted to see how far we'd go," she said.

"The guardian angel?" Andy asked, and he looked at everyone. "Not likely. I'm certain that he's on our side."

"How does he know so much?" she asked.

"He's probably with them, but an objector. You've to admit that these people are not the most well intentioned," said Andy.

She nodded her head. She still had the man's phone on her. They'd dumped all the other phones earlier.

"This is the only way the weak can ever beat the powerful," said Taj. "Every Goliath has to be faced down."

The sound of yelling in the hallway broke their conversation. They all smiled.

"Very well," she said. She didn't know, but slowly something inside her remembered that her father had been a good man, and that he had wanted to correct a wrong in the world.

"Andy," she said. "You'll be in charge of helping me get in and placing the charges. We'll hit right before everything closes. But before people are cleared from the viewing rooms. Taj, you'll be on standby with the homeless men. Drake, you'll be in the getaway car for us in the back."

All of them nodded.

"Andy. You're sure you know where to place the charges?" she asked.

"For the electricity and the back up, yes."

"What about the escape route?"

"I'll show you where to cut the live feeds."

Coral nodded. She felt better now. "Good. You're sure you want to stay?"

"I will. I'll be fine," he said and raised his hands. "Besides, I disappear and they'll come for me."

"Taj?"

"I have a radio, ma'am," he said and held one up.

"Does it work in the area?" she asked.

"I've checked, and it's good to go."

"Okay," she said, her mind clearer now. "Four-thirty, you send in the mob."

The two men left and she stared at the door. There she was, organic material reacting. She thought of all the exponential charts that mass human behavior mimicked so well, and thought of her place in it. Like bacteria in a petri dish. And she was one. Still trying to be an individual, but still part of that chart.

Because no matter the veneer that she tried to apply to the whole of her life, she couldn't help but look at it like that. Like she was swimming against the tide and that she was a fool for doing so. And yet there was that hope wasn't there?

Drake snapped his fingers in front of her. "You all right?"

"I am," she said. "Are you?"

He placed his hands on her shoulders. "Yes."

His alarm woke him up, though he didn't remember turning it on. His shades were down, and it was dark in the room, but he could tell that it was another drab day outside. The smell of Kim's sweat and perfume was embedded in the sheets, and he sighed when he realized that she'd left early again.

He lifted himself out of bed, moving over to the shades, raising them and staring at the world humming along.

In the reflection of the mirror he saw movement and spun just in time to see Coyote with a raised gun.

"What the hell are you doing in here?" asked Matt.

"I could ask you the same thing regarding your unauthorized relationship with a competing organization. Or perhaps I should forward that information to someone in New York?"

For a second Matt's head swooned, could he really afford to deal with this right now? "What are you now, a gossiping teenage girl?"

Coyote chuckled, and tucked his gun away. "So in the interest of sharing information like a saint." He lowered his head at Matt. "I'm here to give something to you."

"And that is?"

"I told you I've got my ears to the street… While you've been busy with your ears to thighs."

"Is this going somewhere?" Matt asked.

"The best people to keep eyes on the streets are criminals. Wouldn't you agree?"

"It's what I taught you." Matt said. He really wanted to say that they were all working for criminals.

"Yet you're not doing it here, are you?"

Matt rolled his eyes, hoping not to be found out. "Are you going to be a child forever?"

Coyote grinned. "Well I've been talking to some criminal types. They say the couriers they use for drugs, usually homeless, have been disappearing lately. Odd stuff."

"Missing homeless people. I'll get right on it."

Coyote raised his hand, palm out, to silence Matt. "I tracked down one of these homeless ones. Druggie. Got him to talk. He's supposed to be ready to go anywhere a guy tells him."

"This is surprising for a junkie?"

"I asked more, and he said he hadn't been told where, though he caught the guy talking about the British Museum. They'd to be well dressed for it. Thrift store tripe, but no rags."

"When?"

"Today, apparently."

"Christ," Matt said. "I wonder what they need the homeless for?"

Coyote shrugged. "I'm guessing it's to do with us, wouldn't you?"

"Sounds like the smart money." Matt's brain raced. Now that it was known, she'd be walking into a trap.

"Do you have an extra pistol?" Matt asked.

Coyote grinned and pulled out his handgun, a 9mm Glock, and threw it on the bed. "You can have that one."

Matt could see the unit signature next to it. "It works, right? Let me find out with this woman that it doesn't."

Coyote tilted his head. "Is the kind one going to shoot the lady? I don't believe it."

"I'm here for a job." Matt tucked the gun into his pants. It felt uncomfortable. He looked Coyote over. "And are you going to come too?"

"Of course. I wouldn't miss this for the world." Coyote turned to leave.

"Coyote," Matt said.

"What?" Coyote said, the door half open.

Matt thought better of his initial thoughts. "I'll call when I get her exact whereabouts."

Coyote nodded and walked out.

Matt wanted to sleep and forget all about this mess. He remembered his father and mother tell him that working hard would always get you someplace in the world. That seemed too foreign to the world that Matt saw now. He thought about the times when his father also said that there were good men and bad. But the bad only won when the good failed to do anything.

Matt would try to be the good man who fought until the end. Though he didn't really believe that. He was only certain that the things his parents had told him when he was young were things he still wanted to do. Matt dialed his phone and talked for a few seconds. Then he walked out. It would be best to talk to all the security men at the museum to get them ready. He called Kim and had her meet him there.

On the taxi ride over, Matt stared at the cars in front of him, like any traffic in the world. There was a whining in his ears the whole way, and he couldn't hear the radio. Everyone seemed to be wearing gray. Every now and then this was punctuated with a woman of gorgeous proportions. But though something deep inside Matt moved towards the women, stirred up his blood, his frontal lobe would reject them, dismiss them as superficial, and he would grow cold. He knew this had something to do with Kim.

When the taxi stopped in front of the museum, it took everything Matt had to swing his feet out of the car and step on the pavement.

"You forgot to pay!" yelled the taxi driver, staring at him through the opened passenger window.

"Sorry," mumbled Matt, and threw a wad of cash at him. As the taxi inched up to some tourists, Matt went weak at the knees and he braced himself on his thighs. He looked up to help get more air into his lungs, and hopefully his brain. Some tourists, with heavy camera-weaponry slung over their necks, brushed by him. It was a couple, fat, so Matt assumed they were American. The man, his stomach sticking out, and his

171

light brown hair in a crew cut stared at Matt. The woman stared ahead with a dead look in her eyes.

Matt looked over the two of them and his fists clenched. He wasn't certain why. He clenched his teeth and drew deep breaths. The couple walked towards the entrance, paying Matt no heed. Matt hadn't lost his temper since the last time he had returned from a deployment in Iraq. That was years ago. And he couldn't fathom the reasons for this recent outrage. He flexed his muscles, relaxing some more.

He knew very well why he was acting this way. He was about to go face to face with the strongest opponent of his life, and he wasn't sure if he was going to survive. And if he wasn't going to survive, then his parents wouldn't either. How sad. The bloodline he'd known and loved was now going to face extinction. He wondered, in a world of seven billion and counting, how many other families were going to be wiped out and who was going to care?

He knew if he had any chance of surviving the day, that he would need to clear his mind of this tripe. He walked past security. Out of the corner of his eye, he was certain he saw Coyote, though when he looked over, he couldn't see any familiar faces.

"Matt!"

Matt turned to see Kim's beaming face tilted at him. He wasn't sure why she was so happy. And though his heart and spirits were immediately lifted, it didn't last long as he thought about the worldviews that separated them. His heart sank and he forced a smile.

"How's it going?" he said and shook her hand.

She narrowed her eyes at him and leaned in. "Are you okay?"

"I'm fine," he said and looked for the driver. At least *that* man had a worldview that was comforting. "Where's the driver?"

"He's gone for the day. My bosses are actually thinking of

investigating him. It turns out that he might have connections to gangs in New Zealand."

Matt's melancholy turned into anger. "Is that based on anything?"

Kim shrugged. "Who's to know?"

"I would think that an investigative process would require something to get started," Matt said.

"Not in today's world," she said.

Matt's eyes gravitated to the top of her blue blouse, Reminders that he had, and probably still, felt a connection to her body and soul.

She smiled. "You sure you're okay?"

He wondered why she was being so friendly. "I'm fine. So you heard the news?"

"That our infamous crook will be here today?"

Matt nodded, looking around at the security men hidden everywhere. "Someone's hired homeless men to come here. Though, for the life of me, I can't imagine why."

Kim looked around. "I don't see how it will help. You have at least a hundred security men here."

Though some of the men were undercover, Matt wasn't surprised that Kim could point them out. Most of them, hired by his company, were nothing more than ex-infantrymen, their hair still too short, and their looks still too muscular, and their stares still too violent.

"I know," Matt said. "The crook hasn't a chance."

"You sound sad about that," Kim said. "I can't imagine that that you'll keep your job if the crook succeeds?"

"Perhaps not," Matt said. He remembered his parents and he nodded his head. He did need to clear his mind. "Let me show you around to get a better look at the security arrangements."

She walked beside him, and as they headed to the basement, where the security nervous system came together, he couldn't help but think of them as a couple, and wonder if he was willing to let go of the silly ideas and hopes in his head and simply be docile enough for her. He looked over, but that stern look and cold aura had taken over her again. He sighed and walked down the stairs.

"I knew a philosopher once. He told me about a question. The duality of man," said Matt. They brushed past some more men in crew cuts.

Kim didn't say anything.

Matt now felt foolish for even thinking about sharing this, but he had to go on.

"The question concerns a scene that you come upon. You are walking through an unknown forest and you come to an opening. You see a man in a small locked cage. And outside is another man, with the keys, is tormenting the man with a stick. The question is who do you fault?"

They came to the basement floor.

"I suppose I would have to ask what the man in the cage did. Why, what's the answer?" Kim said.

Matt wasn't surprised at Kim's words. Just that she said them. "I don't think there is an answer." He knew it was a rebuff of her opening up to him. But now he knew what had to be done. And in the end, the driver was right.

"What happens once we get the homeless men in there?" Drake asked.

Coral smiled at him and chuckled. "We pray."

"Come on," he said. They were in the car, parked about five minutes away from the museum. Coral felt calm, and at peace with what was going to happen, but Drake seemed to be growing nervous. He leaned over, and she kissed him. She wondered if there was a future between them once the rush of this heist was over.

He still seemed nervous.

Coral smiled. She liked that he was so vulnerable.

"We'll be fine."

He nodded, like he wanted to believe her.

"And you're taking that phone?" Drake said.

"*You're* worried about it now?"

"Yeah. I can't believe in someone on their side's trying to help us. What if it's a trap?"

"Those are the risks." She fumbled through her pocket for the phone. She wondered if she was going to trust the voice on the phone. Whoever it was, he had called an hour ago and told her the killer of her father was in the museum. He'd have give her more information if he got it, but he was being watched.

The radio cackled. It was Andy. Three beeps followed.

"Well, this is it," Drake said and started the car.

Coral's mind cleared. She could hear her heart beating, and could smell Drake's cologne. This was it, and she suddenly felt like she was not going to make it. She looked over at Drake. His eyes were focused on the road ahead. She toughened her heart. This was how it was to be. One doesn't worry about their fate, one only marches ahead.

They parked in a dark alley. She would have to go underground from here. She opened the door. The cold outside frightened her, but she pushed forward. She felt Drake grab her wrist.

"Coral. I know you'll be fine. But if anything happens... I just want to say that you have my heart. I wouldn't want to share any more moments with anyone but you."

Her heart jumped and she smiled. "Aren't you the honey-dripper."

Drake smiled, but his face was tense. "I mean it."

"And I feel the same," she said. They kissed. She pulled away before she started to grow weak at the knees. She grabbed her backpack from the trunk. It seemed more off balance than she remembered. She lifted up the heavy sewer lid, the cold and wet steel hurt her fingers, and she slid in. She could see the car move away.

A few minutes later she was at a grated gate.

"Coral?"

Her heart beating fast, and her head spinning, she turned. Andy was standing seven feet from her, flashing the ground in front of him. She couldn't believe that she hadn't seen him. She'd have to be more careful.

"Andy," she said and she felt his hand, leathery and wrinkled, grip her. It should have been comforting, because she could see him place a finger to her lips and he was smiling, a few of his teeth caught in the light of his torch, but she felt a fear that she didn't truly know him, nor any of these people who were her heist team. She followed Andy, her mind turning in anguish.

The rules, these strangers. Was she being weak and foolish to trust them? When she was going up against a billionaire who could very easily buy one of these stranger's dreams and all they had to do was turn her, a stranger, in. She felt cold and shivered. They made it to a door, where Andy slid a card, a light turned green, and they were in a lit hallway.

"Where are we?" she asked.

"Museum basement. We can't have you seen," Andy said, shuffling his feet to a door and sliding his card through its lock. The light flashed red.

Some voices echoed from around the corner, heels clicked. Coral could feel her heart in her throat, but she felt better now that she could see Andy.

Andy slid his card through again and jiggled the door handle. The voices and heels clicks were getting louder. "Bloody hell," said Andy. "We *cannot* have you seen."

Coral kept her eye on the corner. The two men coming nearer were laughing. They sounded terse, like security men.

Her mind stared at the tiles, wondering who put them there, and also wondering how life would've been if she'd been an architect.

"Come."

She felt Andy's hand on her wrist, and she was pulled into a dark room. The light from the hallway cut off as Andy leaned on the door to shut it. The voices and the heels turned the corner and grew louder, then diffused as they walked by. Coral, feeling her blood pressure decrease, took long deep breaths to calm herself down. She could smell pine aerosols in here. And something else she couldn't quite put her finger on.

When nothing but silent echoes remained in the hallway, Andy switched on a light. It flickered before lighting the room in white.

"Oh my," said Coral. They were in a storage room. The other smell must have been the combination of musty smells from artifacts hundreds of years old. Air and bacteria and germs from all places and times mixing together. That calmed her down.

"Give me the charges," Andy said.

"I'm supposed to place them," she said.

"I have enough experience to do it," Andy said, not looking her in the eye. "I didn't tell you, but your picture is plastered everywhere. As soon as someone sees you, you're going to be taken in. They've even questioned three women in the past hour for the crime of looking almost like you."

Coral again felt her blood pressure rising. If they were

that worried, wouldn't they just shut down the whole show? Or was Andy lying to her, to get his hands on the one thing she had that could cause a lot of harm. She looked at him, and he smiled. She really didn't have a choice, did she?

"Are there any cameras in here?" she asked.

"No," he said, as he took the backpack from her.

"You sure you know how?" she asked.

"I've done this before. What do the Americans say? This isn't my first jamboree?"

Coral smiled, though she still didn't like giving up this much control.

"Besides, you're going to need time for the approach."

"Why's that?"

"They have all the vents sealed. There's no way to get in them."

Coral's heart dropped. That had been her plan to get close to the oil-magnate's artifacts. "Are you serious?"

"Does ol' Andy ever lie?"

She laughed. "Fine. So what's the alternative?"

"Maintenance. Towards the end of the business day, a janitor comes around to clean up. You can enter just in time to do what you need."

"Where's the real janitor?"

"No one knows the janitors here."

"And what do I do to look like a janitor?"

"You have the punk look. That should suffice."

"Are you serious?"

"Of course. Plenty of our janitors are workers who come through the juvenile or prison system."

"Really?"

"That's right. All of them, in fact. It's cheap labor for us, and it makes us look like we're doing something honorable."

"Don't they keep an eye on them?"

"Not really. Most are pretty docile. It's how they're picked."

"And how many get on the floors?"

"At least twenty. And you'll be able to blend in." Andy pointed at the cleaner's cart in the corner. "Load her up with what you need."

"I'll go through a maintenance door, then how do I come back in?"

"I'll let you in. Five minutes is all you have. All right?"

Coral tried to think of all the contingencies to this new plan.

They double-checked their watches.

"It'll take no more than three minutes to get to the maintenance door," Andy said.

Coral nodded, trying to remember, but the stress was turning the words into ones without meaning. All she could smell was tofu on Andy's breath. Andy handed her an ID. "This will get you to the door. It may take a few swipes, so don't freak out."

"Whose is it?" Coral asked, staring at the young woman on it who seemed to snarl at the camera as her pale skin shined, and highlighted a scar on her face. For some reason, Coral felt an attachment to the woman.

"She works here, but took to being sick for the week. She might get the ax. But until then, I have her ID."

"You stole it?" Coral asked.

Andy furrowed his forehead. "I did," he said, regret tainting his voice. "But she won't miss it."

"If she gets the blame?" Coral asked. Because as much as this mission meant to her, it seemed pointless to have innocents harmed.

Andy looked down at his hands. "She'll be fine. No one will blame her."

"And what about you?" Coral asked. The rational part of her didn't believe that the woman on the ID would be left alone, but since she needed to believe it, she decided to trust Andy.

Andy shuffled for a few seconds.

Suddenly footsteps ran down the hallway towards them. Coral froze, her hand grasping Andy's. Her heart bounced about in her chest and as the footsteps came by the door, she remembered the handgun and reached for it.

The footsteps ran away from the door and dissipated. Coral's body relaxed and she felt foolish for being so edgy.

Andy coughed. She realized that she was gripping his wrist tightly. She let go and thought about apologizing, though Andy seemed to adjust his collar and coughed again to indicate that it was all right.

"So back to what needs to be done. Soon. Turn left out of this door, then left on the first hallway. Keep your eyes down and here," Andy shoved some earphones into her hands. "Bob your head and ignore anyone." He grinned, as if remembering something.

She nodded and slipped on the earphones. She put in the small earpiece for the radio. "How will it fit?"

Andy looked as she smashed in the earphones.

"Here," he said and handed her superglue.

She stared at him. "Are you kidding me?"

"It'll get the job done. What else is there?"

She thought, hoping to think of something that would work, but she couldn't.

She grabbed the superglue.

"It'll stay, and only rip off a little flesh," Andy said.

She wished that he hadn't said that.

"Thanks," she said, though she was angry. She squeezed out a small drop on the earphones. The sharp pungent smell filled her nostrils, and she held the earphone on the inside of her ear. The superglue worked its magic as it gripped and tightened around her skin. Half a minute later and she let go of the piece. It was stuck. She tapped it slightly. It was sealed for now. She looked at Andy, who stopped grinning.

"I'll head out," Andy said.

"You remember where to place them?" she asked.

"The main electrical lines, to the grid and the generator, and the main and backup fiber cables for the cameras. You have the goggles?"

He was referring to the night vision. "Yes I do," she said. Her mind was tightening, and she couldn't think straight, but she tried her hardest to think of the myriad of ways this mission could go wrong.

Andy waited for something from her, but when she remained silent, he nodded and left.

The door closed, and she was alone in the room. The few items she'd need, she placed in the janitor's cart. It was a long cart, with shelves for cleaners in the front, and a garbage can in the back. The goggles she placed underneath the garbage bag, as well as the kit to break into the cases for the artifacts. There were two she needed to grab. A Greek statue, and a intricate box from the gothic period. That one, from a few interviews in business magazines, she knew to be the one the oil-magnate was most attached to. The gun, the one tool she hoped not to use, she taped underneath the garbage bag, near the top. She tore a small hole in the garbage back so she could reach into it. She threw some paper towels into the garbage bag to cover up the hole.

Her throat tightened, but she slipped into the uniform Andy had left folded on the cart. This was going to be tough, and damn near impossible. She knew that much. And she also knew that the time for second thoughts was over. She remembered the view of the house, charred. And the phone call from Alexandros. She could taste blood in her mouth.

She placed her ear on the door and listened. No one was around. She pushed open the door and entered the hallway. Taking deep, slow breaths, she lumbered down the hallway, bobbing her head. She tried to think of what the woman in the ID would say if some security man confronted her.

Heels came at her, and around the corner. She heard the

hesitation, like the man was taking a longer step to see her better. But the man passed her and walked on down the hallway. She turned into the final hallway. She blasted the music. Heels echoed behind her. They stopped. She could feel someone's eyes on her. The heels came at her. She bobbed her head, hoping that it would save her. What was she going to do if she was caught this early? There really wasn't much. Her hand went into the garbage bag; she touched the edge of the pistol grip.

A strong hand gripped her shoulder. She could feel her skin flush with blood, and a whining sound in her ear. She reached further, gripping the pistol grip. A shot now might destroy the entire plan, but it might also be her only way to freedom.

"Where are the paper towels?" the man asked in an American accent.

She shrugged off the hand and in her best cockney accent said: "Get your man paws off me." She looked the man, who was at least a foot taller, dead in the eye. "You hear me you yob?"

The man, with hard brown eyes, took a step back. He looked confused. "My bad, I just had to clean up a mess."

She threw a roll of paper towels at him. "Take it and go. You try and stop me whilst I work and I'll cut your bollocks off."

The man's chest puffed out, though he seemed to be caught between amusement and fear. "All right. Take it easy." Then a flash of attraction glinted off his eyes.

Coral did her most not to roll her eyes. So he liked being treated rough, did he?

"I'm sorry," the man said. "It's not like your job's the only tough one."

She took the moment to look him up and down, knowing that he would construe it as mutual affection. He'd a side arm, and a security badge. She was certain he was one of the

Texan's minions. "Oh? And what's so tough about your job? You stand around and look hard with a gun?" She flashed a smile to make sure that she didn't lose his attention.

"Well, that's not it. I have to watch for thieves and all," he said, clearing his throat and standing taller.

"How hard is that? Who's so dumb as to rob one of these old pieces of trash."

He laughed. "Well, old pieces of trash they may be, but they're worth a lot. And people do try to rob 'em." He stuck out his chest again and placed his hand on his gun.

"Oh don't be silly and think you can play the cowboy with me. Who's robbing *this* place?"

"Believe it or not," he said, looking around then leaning in. "Someone's trying to rob this place as we speak."

Her heart jumped. "Right now?" she said and looked around. "I don't see anyone." She narrowed her eyes at him.

"Well, not now now, but today or tomorrow."

"For pieces of old trash?"

"That's right," he said and chuckled. "And I'm going to have to stop it."

She smiled and gripped his arm. "Is that right? Don't go hurting yourself."

"I'll be fine. I've seen worse. And it's the thief who needs to watch out. There're plenty of us out here waiting for her."

"Oh, you were in the war?" she asked.

"Iraq and Afghanistan."

She nodded and looked him up and down. "Well, you'd better get going," she said, remembering her own time hack.

He smiled and took a step, then turned. "And your name?"

She tried to remember her ID information, but couldn't. "Yana. You?"

"Brad."

"Don't be thinking I'm easy now."

"I won't," he said. "You'd better not think I'm easy

either."

"Oh?" she said and slapped his ass.

His face froze, then he grinned, blushing. "Take care," he said.

He disappeared around the hallway, and Coral looked at her watch. Less than a minute. She pushed her cart towards the door. Why hadn't she heard anything on the radio? Andy and Taj were supposed to check in, weren't they? She double-checked her watch. Twenty seconds. Was everything going to go wrong? She came up to the door and slid her card through it. It beeped red. She did it again. Again it beeped back red. Now she was certain that everything was going to hell. She leaned against the door, but she couldn't hear anything from the other side.

After Matt showed Kim all the security cameras and the main hub, he walked her back up to the main room.

"How do you think she'll hit it?" Kim asked.

She was still cold, and especially after he'd been foolish enough to ask that philosophical question. But perhaps a cold professional relationship was going to be the best he could do at this age.

"I don't know," Matt said. "I can see how she'll hit us with confusion. But perhaps..." He scanned the room and thought about how he would hit this place. "Maybe she's just out to damage," he said.

"What do you mean?" she asked.

"That she'll have bums rush here, and knock down these cases. Some of them are very fragile."

Kim stared at the statues and lock boxes. "That doesn't seem to fit her profile."

"Neither is having her father killed," Matt said. He bit his tongue when he realized that there was malice was in his voice.

Kim looked him up and down. "You're good at what you do, Matt. But you're too philosophical for this line of work."

That hit him hard; he couldn't see why he liked her. He stared at the ground then looked around. It was near closing time. Perhaps it wasn't going to happen tonight. Kim asked him something and though he wanted to reply, he shrugged instead. He glanced over the crowd. An announcement came over the loudspeaker that the museum goers needed to start heading out. The room cleared. Perhaps this wasn't going to happen. He felt both elated and sad. His phone rang.

"Hi," said Coyote.

"Hey," Matt said. "You in the museum?" He could see Kim look up at him.

"Of course."

"Where's our game?" Matt said, remembering to be tough.

"She'll be here. That cunt wouldn't give up this chance

for the world."

"Listen, I've read into her file, and I think I know where she'll be," Matt said.

"She'll be in the room you're in, because that's her quarry."

"I know that, but she's expecting us then," Matt replied. He thought of how to convince Coyote. "Remember Iraq. The best time to hit someone is when they're ex-filing, right?"

"...Right."

"Then we'll do that. And I'm certain I know where that's going to be."

Coyote didn't reply.

"Do you know where the door to the basement is?" Matt asked.

Before he could hear a reply, a tumult when up. Matt looked up to see the room crowded, with everyone talking loudly at the same time. A thud shook the room, and the lights went out and Matt felt Kim's hand grab his.

Coral stared at the door, shocked that the door just wouldn't open. She touched her earpiece, wondering if superglue had somehow leaked in and rendered it useless. She turned down her music and sighed. She glanced at her watch and realized that it was past the time for the lights to go off. Oh Andy, did you forget? She felt sad, then grew angry at the old man.

"Do you need some help?"

She almost jumped back, and there was Brad, standing tall. She flashed a smile and watched as he smiled back.

"These darn doors," she said and shook her head.

"Yeah, they're a pain." Brad slid his card. The door lock spat out a red light. Brad cussed under his breath and slid the card again. After a few tries it beeped green. Brad nudged the door open slightly. He looked back and grinned.

Coral's earpiece suddenly came alive. She could hear Andy speaking. "All set," said Andy. "Do you hear me?"

"Got it," said Taj.

"Well it's not closing time just yet," said Brad.

"I've got places to be," said Coral, her insides felt knotted. "Besides they see a janitor they leave early."

Brad smiled. Voices cascaded from the room and hit them. Brad's face steeled up. There was a slight vibration in the floor. The lights went out.

"Oh boy. Did they forget their bill?" Coral said, not sure what to do. She could reach for her pistol, but she didn't want to hurt Brad. But she couldn't walk through him, could she?

"No. I think it's the robbery," Brad said.

Coral could sense that his voice had gone cold. He was now a calculating machine. She had no use for that. "Oh no," she said and grabbed his arm. "Are you serious?" She made a point to use the most feminine voice ever. She could smell his cologne, and feel the rising and falling of his breathing.

"Don't worry," Brad said, some warmth returning to his voice.

"You're going to stop them? Be safe," she said, hoping that her words would get him moving, though she half expected him to see through her hyperbolic femininity.

"I will," he said and patted her arm. Then he moved into the room.

Coral pushed the cart into the door to jam it open. The room was loud, and the darkness was punctuated with yells and tussles. A few flashlights were switched on, then fell to the ground. In the beams of light, Coral could see security men wrestling with old men in tweed jackets. She almost smiled. Then remembered her job. She had minutes, if not less. She grabbed her equipment. She could hear a few cases being toppled. There were calls to get the lights. She hoped that the bums, in their obvious glee at being able to do this, hadn't knocked over or damaged the lock box.

She walked the few steps to where the display case was. A man bumped into her, gripped her wrists, then seemed to realize what she was. "Sorry." And ran off. She pulled on her goggles and stared around her. The room had turned into a full-scale fight. She could see more security pouring in from the other rooms. She didn't have much time. She would only get the box. It would be small enough.

Coral walked up to the display case and pulled out her cutting tool. With a quick whir, she cut through the glass case. She looked up, the security men were overwhelming the bums now. She hadn't but a few seconds. She cut through the steel wires and pushed the glass. She pulled out the box. Flashlights were now lighting up the room. She had to get out. She stuffed the box into her uniform and walked to the door. She counted the steps, then pulled off her goggles. Sweat poured down her armpits. She just barely remembered to breathe. Two steps from the door. More flashlights were shining about the room. Then one flashed on the door.

She heard murmurs, and she froze. Would they see her? The gun was in the cart, but if they saw her with a bag, surely they'd know? Then some swear words, and the light turned to darkness. There was more wrestling. Bodies being thrown on the floor. Some security men moaned about the bums' stench. She darted into the hallway and pulled the door shut. Now to get out. She pressed the button in her pocket and spoke.

"Goal. Moving on." She stuffed the bag with her tools and lockbox underneath the garbage bag.

"I'm waiting," Andy said.

She'd have to leave the cart, but not yet. There were flashlights running up and down the hallway. She turned, pushing the cart and feeling the urge to urinate growing. Suddenly a flashlight blinded her.

"Where the hell do you think you're going sweetheart?"

She shielded her face. "Who the hell do you think you are? Get that thing out of my face."

She could feel the hesitation in the man, but it was soon joined by a bullying voice. "We're to keep track of everyone. So come with me."

"Hey," said another gruff voice behind her. "Leave her be."

"What?" Coral's confronter said.

"Brad," Coral said, using her sweet voice again. "Is this your friend?"

"Sorry Yana. He's a bit of a brute," said Brad.

As Brad walked next to her, she grazed his arm. She could feel him stiffen at her touch. She suppressed a smile.

"Tell him to stop flashing that light in my face, 'fore I stuff it into his arse."

"Come on, Jeff. Don't be such a dick," Brad said. The other man lowered his flashlight, though he didn't apologize.

Coral felt her throat tighten as she realized that she may be caught. How else was she going to get out of this situation? Brad wasn't going to be sweet forever.

A radio, on Brad's hip, cackled something incoherent.

"They want us in the display room," Brad said.

Coral stayed quiet though she knew that being too quiet would mean they would smell her guilt. "Did they catch him?" she said.

"Not that I know," Brad said.

"We'd better go," the other, still mean sounding man, said.

"Stay here," said Brad.

"I will," Coral said, trying to sound scared.

The two men jogged off. Coral swallowed.

"Where are you?" Andy cackled over her earpiece. "We need to get you out now, before they seal the final exit."

Coral pushed the cart faster. She wondered what she would say to the next security guard who saw her. Brad was long gone now, she was sure of that.

The phone rang and she answered it. It was the man.

"You want the man who killed your father, right?"

"Who is this?" she asked.

"Come to the storage room."

"Which one is that?" she asked.

"Where you got ready."

She paused, wondering how the man could have known.

"Have your weapon at the ready."

Before she could say anything else, the man hung up. She was only a few feet from the door of the storage room and as she walked up to it, she noticed that the lock was smashed in, with the door slightly ajar. She paused. This was foolish. Even if what the man said was true, this was no way to go about it. She didn't have but a few seconds before the museum was completely shut down. The smart money was to get out now. She'd have her revenge on the Texan with this lock box of his. But smart money dissolved in the face of a bubbling rage as she remembered the charred ruins of her father's house. She reached in the garbage bag for her gun.

"Don't move."

She felt the gun pressed against her head. The voice that

spoke was so cold and heartless that she could already picture the bullet breaking her skull and pushing her brain onto the hallway. She wondered if the man could see her hand.

"Pull your hand from the garbage bag. I can see everything."

Coral removed the hand. Her skin was tight with pressure. She felt woozy.

"Step into that room."

She moved, wondering what she was going to do. Was this how it all would end? At least she never gave up. So why was she giving up now? She pushed the door.

A light flashed from across the hallway, and she felt the gun on her head shift away.

"Freeze!" yelled a man on the other end of the flashlight. She dropped to the ground. A flash from above burned her retina. The accompanying bang sent her ears whining. A hot shell landed on her neck. She flicked it off. There was a bang from across the hallway. The man next to her groaned, and fell back. She crawled to the cart and reached for the gun and bag.

On the other end of the hallway, a flashlight lay on the ground. It highlighted a crumpled man's wrinkled uniform. It seemed like Brad, and she felt a pang of regret.

The man next to her was breathing fast and shallow. There was a sweet smell in the air. She didn't have time to think. She could hear other men running down the hallway, yelling. Swords of light punctuated the dark. She took her bag and gun and ran as fast as she could. She turned the corridor just as she heard shouting. She ran harder.

"Where are you?" Andy hissed over the earpiece. She slipped at a corner but came to the door she remembered. Light beams were following her down the hallway.

The door gave way, and Andy let her in, shutting it softly behind her. "You remember the way?" he asked.

She nodded.

"Go," he said.

"Thank you," she said.

"No time." He pushed her.

Footsteps and yelling ran past the door. She knew what Andy was thinking and she ran.

By the time she pulled herself up from the sewer, she was drenched in sweat. She climbed up, the cold air stinging her moist skin, and saw no car. Her heart dropped. Had Drake abandoned her at the last minute?

"Get up," said a voice behind her.

She stood up. The voice of the man sounded familiar.

"Who are you?" she asked.

"No time. The police told your man he couldn't park here. But the cordon is only a block more. Move past it and you'll be fine."

"But my—"

"Don't waste time."

She turned, expecting an order telling her otherwise. But the man was in the shadows. His hand pointed to the chain-linked fence behind them.

"Climb the fence and walk down the alleyway. Your man will be able to pick you up from there. Ditch the gun. You won't need it."

She wasn't certain. The man had his hand out, but it seemed foolish to hand it over to him.

"We don't have time," the man barked. "I have to be back or I'll be a suspect too."

A siren blared by. She handed him the gun and tools. He nodded at the fence. "Hurry. Did you get him?"

"Someone else did," she said.

"Good."

She ran to the chain fence and climbed up and over.

"Anyone there?" she asked over the radio.

She came out to a main street and saw a car flash its lights. She ran over. Inside, she stuffed the lock box into the trunk, and climbed in as Drake drove the car away.

She kissed him, overjoyed that he'd waited. "I thought you were gone," she said.

"What?" he said and screwed up his face. At the next stoplight they kissed again.

They drove a few blocks and pulled into a garage. Taj had set it up. They left the car and drove a motorbike out of London. They took a boat to Ireland from Wales and when the plane to Aruba landed, Coral allowed herself to relax.

On the beach, with Drake by her side, she maneuvered the sale of the lockbox. She still had so many questions and people to thank, but for now she would bask in sun and the warmth of Drake's smile.

The End

About the Author:

Grunn is not of woman born. Well... maybe not. His mother claims otherwise.

Still, he's one of the most exciting and unpredictable pulp writers of our time.

As a child he drew stories. Then he lost his love of tale for a few years.

When he was twenty, he got lost in the wilds of Alaska and injured himself. Running out of food, he wrote letters on the back of torn and worthless topographical maps. Then he wrote a journal. Then a story. He hobbled out of the tundra, starved and crazed.

He recovered, his love for writing rekindled. But it was still something he wrote on the side, in the confines of his room. They were never books to be the seen by others.

Luckily for the world, in the past few years he's taken his stories and laid them upon the altar of public opinion. You can visit his blog at: http://aarongrunn.blogspot.com/

To sign up for Grunn's events and book deals, go here: http://eepurl.com/L9sm5